A PARENT'S GUIDE TO STREET DRUGS

CHICAGO PUBLIC LIBRARY
WRIGHTWOOD - ASHBURN BRANCH
8530 S. KEDZIE 60652

A PARENT'S GUIDE TO STREET DRUGS

EVERYTHING YOU SHOULD KNOW
EVERYTHING YOUR CHILD ALREADY KNOWS

James M. Lang

STONE FOX PUBLISHING

Copyright © 2001 by James M. Lang

All rights reserved. No part of this publication may be reproduced, stored in a retrieval system or transmitted, in any form or by any means, without the prior written permission of the publisher or, in the case of photocopying or other reprographic copying, a license from CANCOPY (Canadian Copyright Licensing Agency), 1 Yonge St., Suite 1900, Toronto, Ontario, Canada, M5E 1E5.

Canadian Cataloguing in Publication Data

Lang, James M., 1966-
   A parents guide to street drugs

Includes bibliographical references.
ISBN 1-895837-24-3

1. Drugs of abuse. 2. Drug abuse. 3. Youth - Drug use. I. Title.

HV5824.Y68L35 2001   362.29'3   C2001-930391-2

The publisher gratefully acknowledges the support of the Canada Council, the Ontario Arts Council and Department of Canadian Heritage through the Book Publishing Industry Development Program.

Printed and bound in Canada

Stone Fox Publishing is an imprint of
Insomniac Press,
192 Spadina Avenue, Suite 403,
Toronto, Ontario, Canada, M5T 2C2
www.stonefoxpublishing.com

Cover and text design: Richard Bingham, Flex Media (Toronto)

A NOTE TO PARENTS

This book is designed to help you recognize the signs that your child may be using drugs. *A Parent's Guide to Street Drugs* is not a medical or legal textbook. It is an informational guide to educate you about the signs and culture around today's underground drug scene.

• • • •
Please Note

If you believe that your child is using drugs, you should contact the appropriate medical or legal authorities. This is not a matter to be taken lightly. Your child is in danger. The information in this book is a guide, not a how-to manual. We have included a list of some important contact information that you should use if you believe your child is addicted to drugs.

We have tried hard to provide you with the most accurate and up-to-date information about street drugs. The nature of the illicit drug trade, though, means that the price and availability of these drugs changes. Because of this, this book should be used for informational purposes only.

The key to keeping your child safe is understanding. If you are more educated about what today's drug culture looks like, you should be able to spot the warning signs before the drugs take over your child's life. In an ideal world, your child would not be exposed to drugs. This, however, is not an ideal world. Please use the information contained in this book to help reduce the dangers of drugs.

CHICAGO PUBLIC LIBRARY
WRIGHTWOOD - ASHBURN BRANCH
8530 S. KEDZIE 60652

ACKNOWLEDGEMENTS

While there were many people and agencies that helped in the writing of this book, the author would like to thank the following in particular for the kind support and information they provided: Sergeant Marc Pearson of the Royal Canadian Mounted Police (RCMP), the public service information staff at the Drug Enforcement Administration (DEA), and Annabel Williams of the Prevention Awareness for Life Program.

• • • •
Thanks

TABLE OF CONTENTS

Introduction 11

What A Parent Needs To Know 13
    The New Drugs 13
    When to Suspect Drug Use 14
    Drug Paraphernalia 16

Clinical Determinations of Drug Abuse 19
    Beating the Tests 19
    False-Positive Results 20

The Drugs Available To Your Child 22
    Drug Categories 22
    Amphetamines & Methamphetamines 24
    Barbiturates 28
    Cocaine and Crack Cocaine 30
    Common Opiates (Morphine, Codeine, Thebaine) 35
    Gamma Hydroxybutyrate (GHB) 38
    Hashish 43
    Heroin 46
    Ketamine 50
    Lysergic Acid Diethylamide (LSD) 52
    Marijuana 55
    MDMA (Ecstasy) 60
    Peyote & Mescaline 64
    Phencyclidine (PCP) 67

Conversation With A Drug Dealer 70

Prevention 74

Confronting Drug Abuse 79

Glossary of Drug Slang, Jargon & 'Street' Terms 77

Notes 102

Bibliography 102

Internet References and Help Lines 106

A PARENT'S GUIDE TO STREET DRUGS

INTRODUCTION

One of the most difficult situations parents can find themselves in is having an unconfirmed suspicion that their children are using illicit drugs. While there are many fine organizations set up to provide support and information to parents who find themselves in this dilemma, the doctors and counselors from these agencies are not going to be in parents' homes at three in the morning when their children return from a party looking or acting odd. At these critical moments a parent is left on their own to decide if their child is using drugs, what drugs they may be on, and how best to deal with this situation.

As most parents are not trained medical professionals, addressing potential drug use is generally difficult and awkward, producing a minefield of possibilities that a parent has to navigate. No matter what, it seems the cards are stacked against the parent. Understanding what is actually going on and addressing the problem correctly seems almost impossible.

- If your child is under the influence of a drug and you fail to address the issue, your silence could be construed as ignorance or consent.
- If you opt to confront your child later and discover that they weren't under the influence, you could be seen as paranoid, pushy or controlling.
- If you accuse your child of using drugs when they are under the influence but name the wrong drug (e.g., accuse them of being on heroin when they're actually using marijuana, or vice versa) you're very likely going to be regarded as misguided and ignorant.

The only real defense a parent has in such a confrontational situation is to become as aware of popular drugs and the drug trade as their child. But in a world where drugs are more popular than ever, where new and more dangerous synthetic drugs are being introduced faster then ever, and where the potency of common marijuana is one hundred times greater than it was in the 1960s, handling a possible drug abuse situation properly seems daunting.

Introduction

This book will introduce to you the new world of street drugs, including information about where they're found, who sells them, how much they cost and what they can do to your child, to make you, as a parent, as streetwise as possible. However, I caution all parents that this is not a medical text book written by a doctor or a health care professional. Any genuine concerns you have should be addressed to one of the sources listed at the back of this book or to your family physician.

Think of this book as a report from the front lines; a handbook for parents who want or need to know what their child is being exposed to on the streets and school yards of North America.

WHAT A PARENT NEEDS TO KNOW

Is your child using drugs? The first two sections will give you the basics about street drugs today, and address some of the main signs of drug use. It is a discussion of the differences between the drugs of today and those of the 1960s; a review of some possible physical behavioral signs of drug use, the various kinds of paraphernalia to look for, and some of the medical tests used to determine drug use.

• • • • •
The new drugs

THE NEW DRUGS

It's important for parents to understand that the drugs available today are *not* the drugs they knew when they were rebellious teens in the 1960s. Today, drugs are a battlefield. The idea of a fun high, or drug rush, that existed in many communities in the 1960s has now been replaced with a cruel and hard ethic of power, money and control. Drugs are no longer about personal "mind expansion" or "experiencing life"; they are an industry, the result of vicious competition between well-financed drug dealers to create the most potent and extreme high that modern pharmacology can create.

Marijuana, once considered the most benign and user-friendly drug of decades past, is now being cultivated and genetically enhanced to produce THC (the active chemical in marijuana) contents several hundred times higher than marijuana found at Woodstock. Put in perspective, this means that a single joint (marijuana cigarette) bought on the street today would be roughly equal to smoking 120 of the joints found on the streets in the 1960s. PCP (phencyclidine, a beige hallucinogenic powder often called angel dust) is far more available now than during the PCP scare of the late 1970s, with the potency and cut (ratio of pure drug to diluting substances) making it far more dangerous than when it was so vehemently opposed by the media as a "death drug".

The concept of harmless experimentation with drugs as a part of growing up is a thing of the past. Today, not only are we more aware of the harmful effects of drug use, but many of the new drug forms are lethal in even small, first time doses. In the school yards and streets kids are dying: they're being killed by a small air bubble in a dirty syringe or a dose of crystal methamphetamine that turned out to be stronger than the last batch. These kids are victims of cocaine that was cut (diluted) with strychnine or heroin that wasn't "cooked" (prepared for injection) right.

It doesn't matter where you live or how safe you feel your child's school is. In fact, the more affluent schools are often targeted by drug dealers who know that they will make more money by selling drugs to children from wealthy families. All school-aged children are at risk, including your own. Every statistic bears this out.

When to suspect

- Drug use among eighth graders has risen 150% over the past five years.
- A reported 5% of high school students use stimulants on a monthly basis, and 10% have done so within the past year.
- LSD (a hallucinogen commonly known as acid) was used by 8.8 % of twelfth graders during the past year according to the report submitted by the Alcohol, Drug Abuse and Mental Health Administration.

WHEN TO SUSPECT DRUG USE

Before any concrete evidence of drug use becomes apparent, there are signs a parent should watch for. They range from physical and behavioral changes to concrete evidence such as drug paraphernalia. Be careful, however: adolescence is also characterized by many of these signs. It is ultimately up to you to decide if these signs are indicative of drug use or are just your child's right to be a teenager. Understanding that you know your child better than anyone and paying attention to their life and activities can help you spot any possible warning signs and determine their significance.

Physical and Behavioral Changes
A change in any of the following may indicate drug use.

1. Physical Appearance While all teenagers go through "stages" where they become involved in one trend or another, there are certain physical signs to watch for amid the myriad of hairstyles, clothing, and accessories that kids go through. These include

- Red eyes
- Drop in cleanliness, inattention to personal grooming

- Rapid weight loss
- Bruising or scarring, particularly on the arms
- Very pale or red skin coloring
- Increased body temperature

2. School Performance Low grades, recurring tardiness, absenteeism, falling asleep in class, and discipline problems often accompany the onset of drug use.

3. Social Circle Watch for a drastic change in who your child hangs around with. Also, watch any new friends for the same signs. Take notice of your child's and their friends' jewelry or pendants to see if they are wearing drug paraphernalia, such as "roach clips" (small clips used to hold joints), coke spoons (kitchen spoons used to prepare heroin or cocaine for injection), et cetera.

4. Behavior Drug abuse is often characterized by

- Mood swings
- Depression
- Hostility
- Loss of interest in favorite hobbies or pastimes
- A familiarity with drugs, drug terms or expressions
- Lying

Physical Evidence

Physical evidence is often a better indicator of drug abuse. Pay attention to your senses of smell and sight to help you spot any of the physical signs of possible drug use.

1. Unusual Smells Many drugs can be smoked—for example, marijuana, hashish and crack cocaine. The most common and probably the most identifiable scent to be aware of is the pungent smell of marijuana. When burned, it smells similar to burning oregano, distinctly different from cigarette smoke. It is important to note that other drugs may be added to marijuana, either by the user or by the drug dealer, so you may be smelling only half the story.

Because the smell of burning drugs can be quite powerful, many users will try to mask the smell with air fresheners, heavy perfumes or incense. Investigate if your child suddenly starts to use these items. And, of course, heavy scents such as burning drugs and incense tend to linger on clothing, bags or similar objects that have been exposed to the smoke. If your child's clothing or car smells suspicious, there is a possibility that they have been exposed to drugs.

Drug paraphernalia

2. Drug Paraphernalia One of the most obvious clues to drug use or addiction is the paraphernalia that accompanies drug use. While there are a lot of illicit substances that can be used without the use of props (the tools and equipment used to take drugs) many of the most popular recreational drugs require that the user have access to certain specially designed items that aid in the process. Chapter 62 of the Controlled Substances Act (CSA) defines drug paraphernalia as follows:

DRUG PARAPHERNALIA shall mean equipment, a product, or a material of any kind that is used or intended for use in planting, propagating, cultivating, growing, harvesting, manufacturing, compounding, converting, producing, processing, preparing, testing, analyzing, packaging, repackaging, storing, containing, or concealing a controlled substance in violation of Compiled Laws, Section 333.7401 et seq. or in injecting, ingesting, inhaling or otherwise introducing into the human body a controlled substance in violation of Compiled Laws, Section 333.7401 et seq. [1]

The CSA legislation is a standard interpretation of what constitutes drug paraphernalia. Though it is constantly being challenged by pro-drug activists, it remains the legal mandate for what is considered illegal under the CSA. Some of the items listed below are considered illegal under the CSA, others are not, but all are considered to be indicative of drug use.

- *Scale or balance* These are used or intended for use in weighing or measuring a controlled substance. A scale or balance is generally 1 to 2 inches long and hangs from a key chain.
- *Blender or coffee grinder* These are often used to grind raw marijuana into a finer substance that's easier to roll into a joint. These will most likely be kept in the child's room.
- *Small containers* A capsule, balloon, small envelope or other container that can hold only a small amount of a substance.

- *Needles* A hypodermic syringe and needles can be used for injecting drugs such as heroin, cocaine or amphetamines.
- *Pipes* A bong is an elaborate pipe designed for burning and inhaling marijuana, cocaine, hashish or hashish oil. A hash pipe can be made of metal, wood, acrylic, glass, stone, plastic or ceramic. It is usually small (about 3 inches long) and has a permanent screen attached to the bowl.
- *Smoking mask* This is usually a converted World War II gas mask, with what might look like an ashtray attached to the base of the mask.
- *A "kit"* Paraphernalia common to heroin and sometimes cocaine users, a kit is a small pouch containing syringes, alcohol swabs, a spoon or copper bowl, and a propane or butane powered mini-stove, or a lighter, called a "cooker". These are used to prepare some drugs for injection.

• • • • •
Drug paraphernalia

This is only a short list of the many drug-related paraphernalia available. As you can see these items are not exotic or difficult to find. Although police forces work extremely hard to keep these kinds of items out of the hands of children, head shops (small stores that specialize in drug paraphernalia) keep challenging the legality of selling various drug props. Often, well executed and fruitful police raids of head shops result in all charges being dropped before court action is taken. When and if action is taken, the defense invariably challenges the legislation based on constitutional laws that were obviously not designed to address the drug paraphernalia being distributed in these shops. If there are head shops in your community, discuss this with your children. Make sure your children are fully aware of your condemnation of these stores, and let them know they shouldn't frequent these shops.

Unfortunately, this is not enough to stay the flood of illicit drug-related material sold in North America. Nowadays, most head shops have moved off the streets and onto the Internet. Below is a list of links that may allow you to glean more information about drug paraphernalia. Each site is a head shop, advertising on the Web for mail-order business. I recommend that you check out at least one of these sites. There are full-color pictures of various products on each site that will help you identify various kinds of drug paraphernalia.

Drug paraphernalia

http://www.the-head-shop.co.uk/bongs.htm
http://www.marijuana-hemp.com /1010420/Head_Shops/ Smoking_Accessories/
http://www.mtraders.com/html/graffix.html
http://www.bongshop.co.uk/main.htm
http://www.head-different.de/
http://home.earthlink.net/~artzzz/bongs.html
http://www.users.skynet.be/sky68227/dimitri/bong/bong.html
http://www.middleearth69.com/

CLINICAL DETERMINATIONS OF DRUG ABUSE

If you suspect your child of drug abuse, a medical professional has access to a wide variety of tests that go far beyond the superficial evidence available to a parent. It's important to understand that in most places these tests cannot be administered without the consent of the adult or minor to be tested. If you suspect your child of drug abuse, talk to your family doctor to decide whether these tests are appropriate and what the legality is in administering these tests in your area.

• • • •
Beating drug tests

The most common tests for drug abuse use radioimmunoassays (RIA), enzymatic immunoassay (EIA), fluorescence polarization immunoassay (FPI), or thin-layer chromatography (TLC) to measure concentrations of specific drugs in urine specimens. These tests are generally considered 99% accurate in detecting of a specific drug; however, the process depends greatly on when the drug was used and the urinary excretion of drug metabolites. Marijuana may be detected for up to 14 days after repeated use, however, evidence of cocaine, opiates, amphetamines and barbiturates is present for only two to four days.

BEATING THE TESTS

You should be aware that there are ways to beat urine tests. There are a battery of proven methods to throw off the results for any drug user who is actively trying to disguise their habit. A few methods are listed below.

1. *Water Flushing and Diuretics* The test subject ingests a large quantity of water in the hours preceding the test. They will urinate before the test sample is taken to effectively wash out a large portion of the drug metabolites before the test is performed, thus the test sample will register as metabolite-free.

Diuretics are drugs which increase the discharge of urine. Again, the test subject will ingest a diuretic in the hours preceding the test, and flush the system by urinating before the test sample is taken, eliminating a large amount of the drug metabolites.

False-positive tests

2. Ingestion of Interfering Substances The most common interfering substance that a test subject may ingest prior to the test is the poppy seed. While poppy seeds are legal and healthy, they can falsely register as an opiate (a drug derived from the opium poppy) in the user's system (this is called a cross-reaction). Eating a large amount of poppy seeds may corrupt the test results, registering a false-positive result. Claiming interference of another substance provides the user with a viable excuse for a positive test result.

2. Adulterated Urine Samples Because it is extremely important that the samples be genuine, the test subject must be monitored to ensure authenticity. This literally means that either the parent or the health care technician have to see the stream of urine pass from the subject to the specimen bottle. Urine tests have routinely been falsified by subjects obtaining "clean", or drug-free, urine from a friend who does not abuse drugs, then substituting this urine for their own. In many cases this can be done in the presence of the test administrator. The subject can attach a small tube (roughly 1/8 inch in diameter) to the end of a water bottle containing the clean urine, and place bottle and tube between their legs. The urine can then be released through the hose as the subject contracts their leg muscles to squeeze the bottle, thus giving the impression of urination. To avoid this kind of test corruption, the temperature of the urine sample is taken as soon as it is provided. If the temperature of the sample is cooler than the subject's body temperature, it is assumed that the test was corrupted and a new sample is requested.

It's important to understand that tests do not distinguish between occasional users and addicts. Test results will only show if a drug is present in the body. It is up to the parent and the health care professional to follow up with counseling to establish the extent of drug use in the child's life.

FALSE-POSITIVE RESULTS

False-positive results are the bane of the medical professionals who work to detect illicit drug use. While we would all like these tests to be 100% accurate, a false reading is possible even when the subject and the test administrator have both been honest and diligent. A false-positive result is where the urine test reports an illicit drug that was not actually in the subject's system.

False-positive results happen for a variety of uncontrollable reasons. One of the most common reasons is the cross-reaction. A cross-reaction means that the test reacted with medications in the subject's system, or that it reacted with naturally occurring compounds in foods. To prevent falsely implicating the test subject as a user of illegal drugs, screen-positive samples are usually confirmed with more specific (and expensive) techniques such as gas chromatography-mass spectroscopy (GC-MS). These procedures reduce, but do not eliminate, the possibility of false-positive results due to cross-reactions, contamination or mislabeled specimens. Proficiency testing of nearly 1,500 urine specimens sent to 31 U.S. laboratories produced no false-positive results and 3% false-negative results. A similar study of 120 clinical laboratories in the U.K. demonstrated higher error rates (4% false-positive, 8% false-negative), mostly due to laboratories that did not use confirmatory tests.

•••••
False-positive tests

THE DRUGS AVAILABLE TO YOUR CHILD

• • • •
Drug types

The following pages contain information on the drugs your child is likely to encounter at school or through their social circle. Each drug in this section has been selected because of its popularity with children between the ages of 12 and 19. The first section provides an overview of the four main categories that each of these drugs falls into and the effects they produce.

DRUG CATEGORIES

Drugs are medically and legally classified according to their properties and effects. There are four main categories of drugs: stimulants, depressants, hallucinogens and narcotics.

1. Stimulants Often called uppers, these are drugs that stimulate, or speed up, the nervous system, resulting in an increase in energy, heart rate and blood pressure. Stimulants also speed up the metabolism and bodily movements, and increase body temperature. Caffeine is an example of a common stimulant. Some examples of commonly abused stimulants are amphetamines and methamphetamines, cocaine, ketamine and MDMA (ecstasy).

2. Depressants Also known as downers, depressants are drugs that depress, or slow down, the nervous system, causing a decrease in energy, and lowering the heart rate and blood pressure. They slow down the metabolism, relax muscles and can cause drowsiness or sleep. Two categories of depressants are tranquilizers and sedatives. Tranquilizers are mild depressants that produce a calming effect, while sedatives are heavy depressants that are anesthetic, or sleep-inducing. Alcohol is an example of a common depressant. Barbiturates, cannabis (hashish and marijuana) and GHB are examples of commonly abused depressants.

3. Hallucinogens A hallucinogen is a drug that chemically affects the brain, resulting in behavioral changes, visual and aural hallucinations, and the impairment of the perception of space and time. Sensations are enhanced, pain is reduced, and a user may experience an overwhelming combination of color, sound and touch. An overdose may result in psychosis. The cause for the effects produced by hallucinogens are not fully understood. LSD, GHB, mescaline and peyote are examples of commonly abused hallucinogens.

4. Narcotics Narcotics are drugs that relieve both physical and emotion pain. They can induce a dreamlike state of euphoria, and have been used most often in pharmaceutical pain relievers, including cough and allergy medication. Most narcotics are derived from the sap of the opium poppy flower, and include opium, morphine, codeine and heroin. Synthesized narcotics include Demerol and methadone, a drug used to treat heroin addicts. Narcotics are usually highly addictive substances.

● ● ● ● ●
Drug types

AMPHETAMINES AND METHAMPHETAMINES

Classification: stimulants
Common Names: amphetamines, methamphetamines
Street Names: uppers, beans, speed (amphetamines); crank, ice, crystal, meth, crystal meth (crystal methamphetamine)
Chemical or Brand Names: Biphetamine, Desoxyn, Dexedrine, Obetrol
Medical Uses: to treat attention deficit disorder, narcolepsy, obesity
Physical Dependence: high
Psychological Dependence: high
Dose: orally, injected, smoked
Effects: increased alertness, excitation, euphoria, increased pulse rate and blood pressure, insomnia, loss of appetite
Duration of Effects: 2 to 4 hours
Effects of Overdose: agitation, increased body temperature, hallucinations, convulsions, possible death
Withdrawal Symptoms: apathy, long periods of sleep, irritability, depression, disorientation
Approximate Cost per Dose: $20

FACTS

Amphetamines and methamphetamines are lethal and unpredictable chemically manufactured drugs. Like cocaine, they are potent central nervous system stimulants with a high potential to create addicts out of first-time users. As such, they cause an increase in energy and activity, insomnia, and a sense of euphoria, which is why they are called uppers. While amphetamines and methamphetamines are very similar, their chemical structures are different, affecting factors such as the strength and the rate at which the drug is absorbed by the body.

Amphetamines and methamphetamines are usually in the form of a white, bitter-tasting powder, and can be distributed as a powder, pill or liquid. They can be taken orally as a pill, or can be sprinkled in a cigarette or joint (marijuana cigarette) and smoked. The latest and most common form of methamphetamine is crystal methamphetamine, or crystal meth, a chunky, crystallized form of the powder, which is smoked in a pipe.

Crystal Methamphetamine

Often referred to as crank, ice, crystal meth or meth, crystal methamphetamine is a solid, smokable form of methamphetaime. It is also one of the most dangerous and addictive forms of methamphetamine. Use results in a temporary increase in energy and a powerful sense of euphoria. Addiction and habitual use of crystal meth produces a psychotic reaction similar to schizophrenia and the user may experience "tweaking". Tweaking can occur when the meth addict has smoked a steady amount of the drug. The side-effect of insomnia has kept them awake for several days, and as the addict's craving for the drug becomes stronger, they are unable to achieve the high of previous doses, no matter how much meth they take. The frustrated addict, demented from a lack of sleep and the craving, will often become violent. Tweaking is a testament to the crystal methamphetamine's addictive powers.

Amphetamines and methamphetamines, crystal meth in particular, are some of the fastest growing drug problems in the U.S. Many teenagers involved in raves (all-night dance parties) will take these drugs because of the stimulant effects, which keep them awake and dancing for many hours. Amphetamines and methamphetamines have also been known to be abused by pressured students who desire more waking hours to study, and by individuals suffering from the eating disorder, anorexia nervosa.

HISTORY

Amphetamines were originally designed to act as nasal decongestants in the early 1930s. In the Second World War they were liberally distributed to soldiers in Nazi Germany because of their ability to increase metabolism while decreasing appetite. In common medicine, amphetamines and methamphetamines have been used as diet pills, and as a treatment for the sleep disorder narcolepsy. They can also be used to treat hyperactivity and attention deficit disorder because in such cases, the stimulant will act as a depressant, helping the person to relax or focus. The amphetamines and methamphetamines that first hit the streets were mostly from stolen medical supplies. Today, however, they are also produced by illegal labs for specific use as street drugs.

STATISTICS

The 1999 National Household Survey on Drug Abuse (NHSDA) estimated that 9.4 million Americans tried amphetamines or methamphetamines in their lifetime. This figure shows a marked increase from the 1994 estimate of 3.8 million. According to the Drug Abuse Warning Network (DAWN), amphetamine and methamphetamine related emergency department episodes more than tripled between 1991 and 1994, rising from roughly 4,900 to 17,700. Between 1993 and 1995, episodes increased in nine of the 21 metropolitan areas surveyed by DAWN. The number of related episodes more than doubled in Atlanta, Dallas, Denver, Minneapolis and St. Louis. Likewise, treatment providers in California, Oregon, Georgia, Arizona and North Carolina reported significant increases in the number of clients entering treatment with amphetamine or methamphetamine problems.[2]

Crystal Meth Use Among Children
The 1999 Monitoring the Future Survey asked twelfth graders about the use of crystal methamphetamine and found that use had been rising from 1990, peaking in 1998 and leveling off in 1999. Currently, 4.8% of high school seniors have used the drug in their lifetime (compared to 2.7% in 1990), and 1.9% have used it within the past year (compared to 1.3% in 1990). In areas such as the Midwest, where crystal meth is readily available, abuse among teens is much more common. The 1997 Partnership for a Drug-Free America (PDFA) studies found that most teenagers in the U.S. do not see great risk in trying methamphetamine as a stimulant, particularly for recreational use.

WHAT TO WATCH FOR

Some signs that may indicate amphetamine and/or methamphetamine use are listed below.

Physical and Behavioral Signs
- Increased heart rate, high blood pressure and body temperature
- Rapid breathing
- Sweat
- Dilated pupils
- Track marks (needle marks and bruises on the arms from repeated injections)
- Erratic, confused behavior

- Hyperactivity or talkativeness
- Insomnia
- Picking at the skin
- Irritability, violence or tweaking

Paraphernalia
- Crystal meth rocks or amphetamine/methamphetamine powders, pills or liquids
- Hypodermic syringes and needles
- A glass pipe for smoking crystal meth

Amphetamines and methamphetamines

BARBITURATES

Classification: depressant
Common Names: barbiturates
Street Names: barbs, downers, reds, blues, yellows
Chemical or Brand Names: Amytal, Florinal, Nembutal, Seconal, Tuinal
Medical Uses: anesthetic, anticonvulsant, sedative, hypnotic, veterinary euthanasia agent
Physical Dependence: high
Psychological Dependence: high
Dose: orally, injected
Effects: slurred speech, disorientation, drunken behavior without odor of alcohol
Duration of Effects: 6 to 7 hours
Effects of Overdose: shallow respiration, clammy skin, dilated pupils, weak and rapid pulse, coma, possible death
Withdrawal Symptoms: anxiety, insomnia, tremors, delirium, convulsions, possible death
Approximate Cost per Dose: $20

FACTS

Barbiturates are depressants that slow down the nervous system, producing effects that range from mild sedation to coma. These drugs were originally used in medicine as sedatives, hypnotics, anesthetics and anticonvulsants. They are made from barbiturate acid, an organic chemical compound, and were originally created in the 1900s. Barbiturates come as a liquid but are usually prescribed as a pill. The pills come in many colors, hence the street names, reds, blues, and yellows.

There are four classes of barbiturate on the market: ultrashort, short, intermediate and long-acting. These names describe how long it takes for the drug to work and how long the effect lasts.

• *Ultrashort-acting* These barbiturates produce anesthesia immediately after injection. Those in current medical use are methohexital (Brevital), thiamylal (Surital) and thiopental (Pentothal). Abusers prefer ultrashort-acting barbiturates because of the instant high they produce.

- *Short-acting and intermediate-acting* Pentobarbital (Nembutal), secobarbital (Amytal), butalbital (Fiorinal, Fiorice), butabarbital (Butisol), talbutal (Lotusate) and aprobarbital (Alurate) are normally taken orally as a pill and produce a lesser effect over a longer period of time, lasting for up to 6 hours. Short- and intermediate-acting barbiturates are used primarily for sedation in medical practice and by veterinarians for anesthesia and euthanasia of animals.
- *Long-acting* These barbiturates include phenobarbital (Luminal) and mephobarbital (Mebaral). Effects of these drugs are realized in about one hour and last for about 12 hours. Medically, these drugs are used for daytime sedation and the treatment of epilepsy.

Barbiturates are usually taken by teenagers to acquire a euphoric state, or as a depressant to curb the effects produced by another drug.

One of the prime dangers associated with this drug is overdose. Barbiturate intoxication leads to a drowsy, sleepy state wherein the user may not remember how many pills they have taken and can accidentally take a lethal dose. This drug also becomes more potent when taken in combination with alcohol, which can also result in accidental overdose and death.

WHAT TO WATCH FOR

If your child is taking a barbiturate it will be evident in their behavioral pattern almost immediately. Some signs that may indicate barbiturate use are listed below.

Physical and Behavioral Signs
- Excessive sleepiness or long periods of sleep
- Staggered walk (similar to alcohol intoxication)
- Slurred speech
- Track marks (needle marks and bruises on the arms from repeated injections)
- Disorientation
- Mood swings or depression

Paraphernalia
- Hypodermic syringes and needles
- Empty prescription pill containers (especially sleeping medication)

COCAINE AND CRACK COCAINE

• • • • •
Cocaine
Crack Cocaine

Classification: stimulants
Common Names: coke; crack cocaine, crack
Street Names: snow, flake, blow (cocaine); crack, rock (crack cocaine)
Chemical or Brand Names: cocaine hydrochloride
Medical Use: none (cocaine was once used as a local anesthetic)
Physical Dependence: extremely high
Psychological Dependence: extremely high
Dose: snorted, injected, smoked
Effects: increased alertness, excitation, euphoria, increased pulse rate and blood pressure, insomnia, loss of appetite
Duration of Effects: 20 minutes to 1 hour
Effects of Overdose: agitation, paranoia, increased body temperature, hallucinations, convulsions, heart attack, stroke
Withdrawal Symptoms: apathy, long periods of sleep, irritability, depression, disorientation, fidgeting
Approximate Cost per Dose: $20 and up

FACTS

Cocaine is the most potent natural stimulant around. It's extracted from the leaves of the coca plant (*Erythroxylon coca*) indigenous to the Andean highlands of South America. Cocaine produces a stimulant high that is similar to an amphetamine or methamphetamine rush, increasing energy and giving the user a sense of euphoria; yet it can also produce a heightened sense of power, making the user feel invincible. The drug can also produce a numbing effect on the body, similar to a local anesthetic, such as Novocain (please note, cocaine is not currently used in any medical drugs). Cocaine and its derivative drug crack cocaine, or crack, are highly addictive: users can become hooked on the first try, and the craving for the drug increases with each use. Unfortunately for the user, the highs are short-lived, generally lasting under an hour. Because cocaine drugs are so addictive, a user is likely to become violent if they cannot take a dose of the drug.

Cocaine usually comes as a white crystalline powder or in the form of an off-white lump. As with heroin, the color may vary depending on the cut, or purity, of the batch. The most commonly used substance used to cut, or dilute, cocaine is sugar or a sugar derivative. Cocaine can also be reduced into a rock crystal form called crack, which is discussed later in this section.

Powder cocaine is usually snorted, or inhaled up the nose, through a straw or a rolled dollar bill. The cocaine is absorbed into the bloodstream through the nasal tissues. Occasionally, the powder is sprinkled into a joint or a cigarette, and then inhaled along with the marijuana or tobacco smoke. However, injection is the most direct means of taking cocaine: the white powder is "cooked", or reduced to a liquid, and injected directly into the user's vein using a standard hypodermic syringe. The cooking process is used for a wide variety of drugs including heroin, LSD, PCP and many barbiturates. Virtually any powder or pill can be transformed into an indictable liquid using the cooking technique.

Cocaine
Crack Cocaine

Cooking Cocaine
This process sanitizes the cocaine and liquefies it at the same time. Understanding the cooking process is an important part of detecting cocaine use in your home. The following is an outline of the process and the equipment needed to cook cocaine.

1. The white powder is purchased by the gram. Each gram of cocaine is packaged separately in a 1-square-inch bag or elaborate paper fold.
2. The powder is taken out of the bag or paper and placed in a standard kitchen spoon or cooker (a special pan that is 1 inch in diameter).
3. A syringe is then filled to about 20 cubic centimeters with distilled water. This water is squirted into the spoon. The end of the needle is used to mix the water with the cocaine.
4. The spoon is heated with a standard cigarette lighter or a butane powered stove called a burner. The mixture is heated to a quick boil, and the resultant liquid is considered cooked.
5. When cooled the liquid cocaine is drawn into the syringe. Often, a small torn piece of cotton, or possibly a torn piece of an unused cigarette filter is used to filter out dust particles or remaining solids in the liquid.
6. The cooled liquid is injected directly into the user's vein.

Crack Cocaine

Crack and rock are the street names for cocaine which has been processed from cocaine hydrochloride to a ready-to-use freebase, or boiled residue of cut cocaine powder, for smoking. To make the freebase, the cocaine powder is mixed with either ammonia or sodium bicarbonate (baking soda), and water and heated to remove the hydrochloride. The result of this process is a potent, crystallized form cocaine that can be readily smoked with no need for joints or cigarettes.

Crack is smoked in a similar way as crystal methamphetamine: the rock crystals are placed in the bowl of a special glass pipe (a crack pipe) and burned, allowing the user to inhale the smoke. The clear glass pipe is used because the burning rock emits a light-blue flame that can been seen tracing along the neck of the pipe while it is being inhaled. Traces of the baking soda remain in the final product, and when ignited, it emits a crackling sound, hence the street name crack.

Crack is sold in small, inexpensive doses, which accounts for its popularity in low-to-middle-income areas. It effectively delivers the same high as cocaine administered intravenously, without extravagant cost or the need for needles. The effects are felt almost immediately after smoking and are very intense, but do not last long.

HISTORY

The anesthetic properties of cocaine were discovered in the late 1800s, and the drug became commonly used in medical practice as a pain reliever. The famous Austrian neurologist and psychotherapist Sigmund Freud prescribed the drug to a number of his patients. For a short time, cocaine also turned up in a number of common products, including soda pop. However, when the addictive powers of cocaine became apparent, use of the drug was discontinued. Today, cocaine is not used in medicine. Crack cocaine was developed later in the twentieth century as a street drug. Part of the reason for its popularity is because it is considerably less expensive than cocaine, which can be very costly.

STATISTICS

Cocaine is readily available in all North American cities. According to the Office of National Drug Control Policy, cocaine use has been on the rise in San Diego, Bridgeport, Miami and Boston. Despite political and economic incentives by the U.S. federal government, Colombia remains the world's leading source for cocaine, producing three-quarters of the world's annual yield, with a 28% increase in the amount of coca plants in Colombia in 1998. Taking into account crop reductions in Bolivia and Peru, Colombia is the nation with the largest number of acres of coca under cultivation.

From 1991 to 1998, the number of first-time cocaine users had increased 63%, from 574,000 to 934,000 users. Though not as prevalent as it was in the 1980s (cocaine use peaked in 1982 when a reported 10.4 million Americans used cocaine), the number of students reporting use of powder cocaine rose during the 1990s, making cocaine addiction an important concern for parents in North America. In 1991, 2.3% of eighth graders said they had used cocaine and this figure rose to 4.7% in 1999. Among high school students, increases in cocaine use began in 1992 and continued to rise through the beginning of 1999. Between those years, the rate of cocaine use went from 3.3% to 7.7% among tenth graders and from 6.1% to 9.8% among twelfth graders. Use of crack cocaine also increased among eighth, tenth, and twelfth graders, from an average of 2.0% in 1991 to 3.9% in 1999. The 1999 National Household Survey on Drug Abuse (NHSDA) found the highest rate of monthly cocaine use was for those aged 18 to 25 at 1.7%, increasing from 1.2% in 1997.

• • • • •
Cocaine
Crack Cocaine

WHAT TO WATCH FOR

Unlike marijuana or LSD, cocaine can be a solitary drug. In other words, your child need not be going out partying or being social in order to use it. Due to its highly addictive nature, a user can become very solitary and protective of their stash, or supply of the drug. Of course, cocaine can be used by a loner as well as by a socialite. Some signs that may indicate cocaine or crack cocaine use are listed below.

Physical and Behavioral Signs
- Increased heart rate, high blood pressure
- Dilated pupils
- Sweat
- Bloodshot eyes
- Runny nose
- Severe respiratory problems or excessive coughing
- Track marks (needle marks and bruises on the arms from repeat-

ed injections)
- Jerky, frenetic movements (commonly referred to as the "chicken dance") or hyperactivity
- Talkativeness or irrational intensity in discussions
- Paranoia
- Irritability or violence

Cocaine
Crack Cocaine

Paraphernalia
- Empty 1-square-inch plastic or paper packets
- Rolled up dollar bills or short, cut drinking straws (used for snorting)
- A small mirror and razor blade (to divide the cocaine into lines for snorting)
- Hypodermic syringes and needles
- Cocaine cooking equipment (coke spoons, cookers, burners, et cetera)

COMMON OPIATES: MORPHINE, CODEINE AND THEBAINE

Classification: narcotics
Common Names: opiate variant, codeine, morphine, thebaine
Chemical or Brand Names: Duramorph, MS-Contin, Roxanol, Oramorph SR
Street Names: Tylenol with codeine, Empirin with codeine, Robitussin A-C, Fiorinal with codeine, APAP with codeine
Medical Use: analgesic, paregoric
Physical Dependence: extremely high
Psychological Dependence: extremely high
Dose: smoked, orally, snorted, injected
Effects: euphoria, drowsiness, respiratory depression, constricted pupils, nausea, constipation
Duration of Effects: from 15 minutes to 4 hours
Effects of Overdose: slow and shallow breathing, clammy skin, convulsions, coma
Withdrawal Symptoms: watery eyes, runny nose, yawning, loss of appetite, irritability, tremors, panic, cramps, nausea, chills and sweating
Approximate Cost per Dosage: As there are so many opiate variants, costs vary from over-the-counter and prescription prices, to more expensive street drug prices.

● ● ● ● ●
Morphine
Codeine
Thebaine

FACTS

Opiates are narcotics derived from the sap of the opium poppy plant *Paver somniferum,* a particular species native to Asia Minor—not your average garden-variety poppy. Opiates produce a euphoric state and can relieve physical or emotional pain. Common opiates are those used in medicine, such as morphine, codeine and thebaine. While heroin is an opiate, it is not used in medicine; thus it is not considered a common opiate for the purposes of this book, and it is discussed in a separate section.

While there are a few synthetic opiates (e.g., methadone, a drug used to treat heroin addiction), all natural opiates, including morphine, codeine and heroin are derived from opium, a tar-like substance distilled from the sap of the opium poppy, which is found in the bulb of the plant. To extract the sap, opium harvesters use special tools to make an incision on the bulb of the plants. Later, when the poppies come to maturation, a raw, gummy substance oozes from the incisions. This gum is pure opium, and is collected by the harvesters, packaged and sent to be refined into the various types of opiates.

Morphine, Codeine and Thebaine

Morphine
Codeine
Thebaine

Opiates are often prescribed by doctors as pain relievers. They can be taken orally, as a pill or as an ingredient in a medicine syrup. They can also come as a liquid for injection, or in the form of a suppository. Morphine is considered to be a strong opiate, and requires a prescription. It is used to relieve intense pain. While codeine was once used in over-the-counter drugs such as cough syrups, pain relievers and allergy medications, it is also considered to be a strong opiate, and today it also requires a prescription. These types of opiates that are sold on the street are usually stolen pharmaceutical supplies or have been obtained through a fake prescription.

It is important for parents to understand that your child does not necessarily have to be buying opiates on the street because there are very simple ways to extract the opiate constituents from common prescription drugs such as cough medicines and pain relievers using common kitchen utensils and a freezing process. The result of this process will produce an isolated opiate that is as strong as any available on the street. Below is a list of items that may indicate that your child is distilling opiate constituents from common medicines.

- Large numbers of cold remedy bottles containing codeine, morphine or thebaine
- Frozen containers of clear liquid, possibly with a cheesecloth or other filter on top
- Cheesecloth or another kind of fine cloth with crystalline particles on it

Morphine distilled using this process will appear as a glassy, crystalline substance not unlike ground sea salt. You will usually find it attached to the cheesecloth or other filter. It will be slightly acidic in taste, and will fall away from the cloth with a gentle shake.

HISTORY

There were no legal restrictions on the use of opium until the early 1900s. If you had the money, you could purchase any opiate with impunity at your local drug store or five-and-dime. Legislation to prevent the use of opiates arose in the early 1900s in response to a growing epidemic of users, notably in New York City, whose lives were being destroyed by opiate use. Once-prosperous business people were quickly being reduced to penniless addicts. Bereft of funds, many addicts began collecting tin cans and other discarded metal to sell to local smelting plants. The small amount of change they made was used to purchase more opiates, and subsequently this became the backbone of the opiate trade in New York in the late 1800s and early 1900s. The people whose addiction relied so heavily on collecting the discarded metals became known as the "junk collectors" or "junkies". The term junkie is still used today to refer to a person whose addiction has destroyed their life and forced them into menial or illicit work to support their drug habit.

To combat the epidemic of opium addiction in the early 1900s, state, federal and international laws were passed governing the production and distribution of opiates and opiate variants.

• • • • •
Morphine
Codeine
Thebaine

WHAT TO WATCH FOR

Some signs that may indicate opiate use are listed below.

Physical and Behavioral Signs
- Constricted pupils
- Nausea and/or vomiting
- Constipation
- Cramps, chills and sweating
- Runny nose
- Track marks (needle marks and bruises on the arms from repeated injections)
- Euphoria
- Drowsiness

Paraphernalia
- Large numbers of empty cold medicine or prescription drug containers that contain codeine, morphine or thebaine
- Frozen containers of clear liquid covered with a fine cloth
- Hypodermic syringes and needles

GAMMA HYDROXYBUTYRATE (GHB)

Classification: depressant
Common Names: GHB, gamma hydroxybutyrate
Street Names: liquid x, Georgia home boy, goop, gamma-oh
Chemical or Brand Name: gamma hydroxybutyratic acid
Medical Uses: none (GHB was once used as a pre-anesthetic and to treat addiction)
Physical Dependence: none
Psychological Dependence: moderate
Dose: orally
Effects: euphoria, drowsiness, hallucination
Duration of Effects: 2 to 4 hours
Effects of Overdose: fatigue, paranoia, dizziness, nausea, unconsciousness, seizures, severe respiratory depression, coma
Withdrawal Symptoms: none
Cost per Dose: $10 per bottle (approximately 10 doses per bottle)

FACTS

Gamma hydroxybutyrate (GHB) is an isolated carbohydrate that exists in many common foods, among which are beef and poultry. This organic element was originally used to develop a pre-anesthetic drug that worked as a sedative rather than a painkiller. As such, it was used to calm a person before surgery and prepare them for general anesthetic. As a drug, GHB is a central nervous system depressant that produces euphoria and hallucinations.

GHB usually comes as a clear, salty tasting liquid, a white power or as a capsule. The drug's effect is usually experienced within 10 or 15 minutes of ingestion, though this estimate can vary up to an hour depending on the user's metabolism. In small doses, the effect of GHB is allegedly similar to alcohol intoxication, reducing social inhibitions, one of the reasons it is popular as a recreational drug. In higher doses, the drunken euphoria fades and is replaced by a sedative effect roughly equal to that of 10 Valium tablets. Common reactions are nausea, drowsiness, amnesia, vomiting, loss of muscle control, respiratory problems and occasionally loss of consciousness. After excessive use, some users have experienced seizures and coma.

The Date Rape Drug
Because of its anesthetic properties, GHB has become extremely popular as a "date rape drug": it is being used in many social situations as a means to sexually assault an unsuspecting victim without their knowledge. A quantity of the drug is slipped into the drink of an unsuspecting person, perhaps in a bar, club or at a party. The dose will initially produce a euphoric intoxication that the victim will assume is a result of alcohol consumption. While the victim is in a state of euphoria, the rapist is then able to guide the victim away from the bar without suspicion: to the public eye, the victim will seem giddy and happy to be leaving with the assailant, and because of their impaired state, the victim will not know what is happening to them. As the drug's effect intensifies, the victim will enter the anesthetic phase of the drug state wherein they become unconscious. If the assailant has maneuvered the victim into a remote area by the time the anesthetic phase begins, the victim will be entirely vulnerable to the rapist. Moreover, when the victim regains their faculties they are unable to recall what had happened to them while they were under the influence of GHB.

HISTORY

Originally marketed as a natural food supplement, GHB was not only used as a pre-anesthetic, but it was used to treat alcohol addiction and the sleep disorder narcolepsy. GHB was also used in food supplements, as a weight-loss aid, and as a body-building supplement and sold in health food stores. Soon, the medical community became aware that GHB caused health problems, and in 1990, the Food and Drug Administration (FDA) issued an advisory declaring GHB unsafe and illicit except under FDA-approved, physician-supervised protocols. In March 2000, GHB was placed in Schedule I of the Controlled Substances Act, making the drug illegal even as a prescription drug. There is no current legal application for GHB.

Despite laws restricting GHB possession and use, kits containing chemicals and recipes for making GHB are still sold in many stores today. These GHB kits contain non-regulated precursor chemicals (chemicals that can be combined to create GHB but are not individually illegal) that are marketed under various brand names, including Sodium Oxyrate, Sodium Oxybutyrate, Gamma Hydroxybutyric Sodium

Acid, Gamma Hydroxybutyric Sodium, Gamm-OH, 4-Hydroxybutyrate, Gamma Hydrate, Somatomax PM, Somasnit, and Gamma Hidroxibutirato. GHB is still abused as an alternative to anabolic steroids, and abused by for recreational and criminal reasons.

STATISTICS AND GOVERNMENT RESPONSE

According to the Drug Abuse Warning Network (DAWN) GHB-related emergency room visits nationwide increased from 20 in 1992 to an estimated 629 in 1996. The majority of the episodes occurred among 18 to 25 year olds (66%), Caucasians (94%), and males (79%). When a motive for GHB use was reported, 91% of users reported using the drug recreationally. When a reason for the emergency room visit was reported, an overdose was listed in 65% of the episodes and an unexpected reaction was listed in 33%.

Possibly in response to these statistics, the FDA released a White Paper on GHB in 1999, addressing the various health claims regarding the drug.

FDA RE-ISSUES WARNING ON GHB

GHB is a chemical that has been promoted as a steroid alternative for body building and other uses for several years. Recently it has gained favor as a recreational drug because of its intoxicating effects. Although in the past GHB has undergone clinical testing for several indications, it has never been approved for sale as a medical product in this country.

By the end of 1991, FDA and the Department of Justice had taken enforcement action against several firms and individuals involved in manufacturing, distributing and promoting GHB. The agency also instituted an automatic detention policy to prevent products containing GHB from being imported. These actions—along with embargoes, public education campaigns and other measures taken by state and federal authorities—appeared to temporarily diminish the distribution and abuse of GHB.

Recently, however, there appears to be a resurgence in the abuse of GHB: virtually all of the products now encountered have been produced in clandestine laboratories. This increase in use has been accompanied by an increase in reports of GHB-related injuries, including deaths.

Although some promotion schemes occasionally make unlawful

claims that GHB is a legal drug, it is illegal for any person to produce or sell GHB in the U.S. FDA's Office of Criminal Investigations is working with United States Attorneys Offices around the country to arrest, indict and convict individuals responsible for these illegal operations. FDA, the Centers for Disease Control and Prevention and the Drug Enforcement Administration are continuing to monitor GHB abuse and to develop the most effective measures to protect the public health.

Although the FDA and Drug Enforcement Administration (DEA) are resolute in listing GHB as a Schedule I drug, having no legal applications, many states have not yet recognized it as such. Proposed bills to list GHB as an illegal drug are being argued before various state legislatures, but controversy is hampering any efforts to pass them. Of primary concern to lawmakers is the "natural" composition of GHB. As mentioned earlier, GHB is also an isolated carbohydrate that exists in many common foods. According to the guidelines of the FDA, any substance listed in Schedule I of their guidelines is strictly forbidden, and therefore any product containing a Schedule I drug is illegal. However, as GHB is naturally present in many meats, the legislation prohibiting the drug would by legal implication make meat illegal. For this reason, GHB legislation needs to be addressed carefully by lawmakers in order to accommodate natural GHB content in certain foods, while restricting illicit use of the drug.

WHAT TO WATCH FOR

Some signs that may indicate GHB intoxication and use are listed below.

Physical and Behavioral Signs
- Nausea
- Vomiting
- Loss of muscle control
- Drowsiness
- Amnesia
- Drunken behavior, especially when as little as one drink has been ingested
- Low inhibitions
- Blackouts

Paraphernalia
- GHB kit
- Packages of "natural" anti-depressants, body building or weight-loss aids
- Food supplements combining sodium oxyrate or oxybutrate, gamma hydrobutyric, et cetera

HASHISH

Classification: depressant
Street Name: hash
Common Names: hashish, hash, hash oil
Chemical or Brand Name: n/a (active ingredient: delta-9-tetrahydrocannabinol, or THC)
Medicinal Uses: none
Physical Dependence: none
Psychological Dependence: moderate
Dose: smoked, orally
Effects: mild euphoria, drowsiness, increased appetite
Duration of Effects: 1 to 3 hours
Effect of Overdose: fatigue, paranoia, disorientation
Withdrawal Symptoms: insomnia, hyperactivity, decreased appetite
Approximate Cost per Dose: $10 to $20 per gram ($2 per joint)

FACTS

The word hashish has a different meaning all over the world. One thing that all definitions agree on is that it is a derivative of the cannabis plant. However, the cannabis plant is either male or female. The male plant does not produce the intoxicating substance delta-9-tetrahydrocannabinol (THC) that is associated with the plant name. The male plant is used to make rope, building materials and cloth. The female cannabis plant, however, produces seeds and flowering tops, or buds, rich with THC, and is the form of the plant from which marijuana and the drug hash are derived.

Hashish originates as an Arabic word. In Arabic cultures it refers to any product made from either the male or female cannabis plant. Other cultures, however, refer to the products of the innocuous male plant as cannabis, and call the drug resin derived from the THC-rich female plant hashish or hash. In North America, the term hemp is used for any product derived from the male plant, and the terms hashish, hash or hash oil for the THC-rich resin of the female plant.

Hash is a depressant similar to marijuana: the THC causes a feeling of euphoria in the user, as well as drowsiness and an increase in appetite. However, while marijuana is a tobacco-like substance made from the seeds and buds of the female cannabis plant, hash is an extracted resin that is dried and pressed into either a firm, clay-like substance about the consistency of Play-dough, or pressed into an oil.

Hash and hash oil can be smoked or eaten. The method of smoking hash varies.

• *Hash cigarettes* The clay-like hash is broken into small pieces and mixed with tobacco and/or marijuana, rolled into a joint and smoked.
• *Hot knives* Kitchen knives are placed on a burner until the blades are extremely hot. The hash is then dropped on one knife blade and the second blade is used to press the hash between the two hot blades. The user inhales the resultant smoke as it rises from between the blades.
• *Hash pipe* Hash pipes sold in most head shops (small stores that specialize in drug paraphernalia). They are usually fairly ornate pipes about 4 inches in length. A small screen, or piece of wire mesh, sits at the lip of the bowl. The hash is placed on this screen, and a lighter flame is used to ignite it. The user draws deep breaths through the pipe while the hash is burning, inhaling the resultant smoke.

As well, hash and hash oil can be used in baked items, such as "hash brownies". After eating these food items, the THC is slowly absorbed into the bloodstream through the process of digestion.

HISTORY

The refined resin we now call hashish was first introduced to the world in 1092 during the Crusades. Hasan bin Sabah, a Persian convert to the Ismaili sect of Shia Muslims, founded a secret brotherhood sworn to destroy the Abbasid Caliphate of Baghdad and its overlords, the Seljuk Sultans. The brotherhood policy of secretly killing any political opponent was so successful that within 15 years the influence of the brotherhood had spread as far as Syria and Lebanon. The unofficial title given to Hasan bin Sabah was *Sheikh el-Jebel* —the Old Man of the Mountain. The followers of this sect were referred to as "Followers of Hasan", "Hasans", or, as you are more likely to know them, the "Assassins".

One of the religious aspects of the Assassins was the prolific use of THC-rich cannabis before a bombing raid or an assassination. The THC high was reportedly a sign of Allah's favor and an indication of what

When it is further refined, the black tar heroin will solidify, taking on the appearance of coal or a hard licorice candy.

Heroin is not only addictive, but an overdose is always a standard risk, even for the most experienced user. Because the cut (ratio of the amount of pure drug to the amount of diluting substance) varies so dramatically from dose to dose, it is almost impossible to accurately assess the amount of powder needed to achieve the maximum high without crossing the body's tolerance threshold for the drug. Two packets of heroin bought from the same dealer at the same time could require entirely different applications. What may be the right amount for one purchase could easily be an overdose for the next. Users have to rely heavily on hearsay and dealer information to assess the proper amount of heroin to administer in each dose.

Heroin is almost exclusively an intravenous drug. While it can be smoked, snorted or taken orally, it is not commonly administered in this way. It is injected to retain the purity of the drug and to achieve the fastest, most effective high. Heroin users transform the powder drug to a liquid through the cooking method. Because of the significance of intravenous administration, heroin users will usually have kits containing the apparatus designed for heroin use. These kits include a hypodermic syringe and needles; a burner (mini-stove or lighter); a copper cooker, or small pan that is 1 inch in diameter; alcohol swabs; bandages; a tourniquet; a bottle of distilled water; and cotton. These materials are often contained in small wooden boxes the height and width of a pen case, and twice as thick.

Cooking Heroin
This process sanitizes the heroin and liquefies it at the same time. Understanding the cooking process is an important part of detecting heroin use in your home. The following is an outline of the process and the equipment needed to cook heroin.

1. The white powder is purchased by the gram. Each gram of cocaine is packaged separately in a 1-square-inch bag or elaborate paper fold.
2. The powder is taken out of the bag or paper and placed in a standard kitchen spoon or cooker.
3. A syringe is then filled to about 20 cubic centimeters with distilled water. This water is squirted into the spoon. The end of

the needle is used to mix the water with the cocaine.
4. The spoon is heated with a standard cigarette lighter or a burner. The mixture is heated to a quick boil, and the resultant liquid is considered cooked.
5. When cooled, the liquid heroin is drawn into the syringe. Often, a small torn piece of cotton, or possibly a torn piece of an unused cigarette filter is used to filter out dust particles or remaining solids in the liquid.
6. When cooled, the liquid is injected directly into the user's vein.

AVAILABILITY AND STATISTICS

Where you live has a great impact on whether your child is going to be readily confronted with heroin in the schools and streets. While no city is entirely free of the lure of illicit drugs like heroin, there are areas designated by the Drug Enforcement Agency (DEA) as prime locations for heroin use and availability.

Heroin "outlets" exist in many East Coast cities, including New York (the center of Dominican Republic-based criminal groups), Newark, Boston, Baltimore, Philadelphia and Orlando. South American heroin markets are also emerging in Washington, D.C., Atlanta, Miami, Fort Lauderdale, New Orleans, Detroit and Chicago.[3]

The flow of South American heroin began to increase dramatically in 1993 when Colombia-based drug organizations, already in control of the worldwide cocaine market, expanded into the heroin trade. They quickly saturated the U.S. heroin markets through Dominican distribution rings by providing low-cost, high-purity heroin. Now they also employ strategic marketing tactics such as providing free samples of heroin in cocaine shipments in order to build a clientele. They even market their drug using brand names, such as No Way Out and Death Wish, as a way to establish customer recognition and loyalty.

The most recent report of the Drug Abuse Warning Network (DAWN), which tracks drug abuse deaths and emergency room episodes in major U.S. cities, indicated a steady increase in the number of heroin-related deaths from 1992 to 1998. In this study, the number of incidents in which heroin/morphine (these two substances cannot be differentiated once the body metabolizes them) was found in the bloodstream rose from 2,868 in 1992 to 4,327 in 1998.

The 1999 National Household Survey on Drug Abuse (NHSDA) reported an estimated 149,000 new heroin users in 1998 and that nearly 80% of them were under the age of 26. The study also found the number of persons who had used heroin within a month of the survey had increased from 68,000 in 1993 to 208,000 in 1999. The 1999 Monitoring the Future survey found little change between 1996 and 1999 in annual use among tenth and twelfth graders.

SPECIAL CONCERNS
If you have any suspicion that your child has been exposed to heroin, the Drug Abuse Resistance Education (DARE) program advises parents that it is vital that you speak to your child about it immediately. Heroin is highly addictive, and it is essential that you either prevent or stop its abuse as early as possible. Visit their Web site at *www.dare.com*, or contact a local drug counseling center for more information on how to address or confront child drug use.

WATCH TO WATCH FOR
Some signs that may indicate heroin use are listed below.

Physical and Behavioral Signs
- Track marks (needle marks and bruises on the arms from repeated injections)
- Euphoria
- Drowsiness and/or apathy
- Respiratory depression
- Constricted pupils
- Nausea
- Erratic or violent behavior (when the user craves another dose)

Paraphernalia
- Small wooden box the height and width of a pen case, and twice as thick containing equipment for injecting heroin
- Hypodermic syringes and needles
- Burner (mini-stove or lighter)
- Copper cooker (small pan that is 1 inch in diameter) or kitchen spoon
- Alcohol swabs, bandages, a tourniquet, cotton and bottle of distilled water

KETAMINE

Ketamine

Classification: stimulant
Common Name: ketamine
Street Names: special K, K, super acid
Chemical or Brand Name: ketamine hydrochloride
Medical Use: veterinary anesthetic
Physical Dependence: unknown
Psychological Dependence: moderate
Dose: orally, smoked, snorted
Effects: increased alertness, excitation, euphoria, insomnia, hallucinations, loss of appetite, increased pulse rate and blood pressure
Duration of Effects: 1 hour
Effects of Overdose: agitation, paranoia, hallucinations, convulsions, stroke
Withdrawal Symptoms: apathy, irritability, disorientation
Approximate Cost per Dose: $20

FACTS

Ketamine hydrochloride, also known as Special K and K, is a new addition to the list of synthetic street drugs, or "designer drugs". It was only placed in Schedule III of the Controlled Substances Act in August 1999. Ketamine is a combination of a stimulant and a hallucinogen: it both increases the heart rate and energy, and causes a sense of euphoria and hallucinations in the user. (The stimulant effect is similar to PCP and the hallucinogenic effects are close to those of LSD.) Drugs that produce this cross-over effect are the fastest growing drug problems of the new millennium. Ketamine is considered a "club drug", and accordingly, its popularity as rave (an all-night dance party) drug is growing exponentially. Ravers prefer ketamine and drugs like it because the metabolic enhancer, or stimulant, in ketamine shortens the hallucinogenic effect to approximately one hour, thus allowing the user to come down from the effects of the drug before returning home. This effect contrasts directly with the hallucinogenic effect of a drug like LSD, which lasts a minimum of four hours, and can remain in the system for days. The amphetamine also increases the user's energy level, allowing them to remain awake all night, energized for dancing.

While the hallucinogenic effect is short lived, ketamine's other effects remain with the user for up to 20 hours. Judgment, coordination, and the ability to interpret sensual input are severely distorted. For this reason it is advisable to prevent a suspected ketamine user from driving within 24 hours of use.

Ketamine comes in the form of a powder, pill or liquid. It is generally taken orally by placing it in a beverage, and it can also be added to marijuana, in a joint, and smoked. As a powder, ketamine is white, resembling cocaine and baking soda, and can be snorted.

HISTORY

Ketamine was developed in the 1970s as an anesthetic for humans and animals. It soon fell out of use for humans, but it is still used by veterinarians. For this reason, original doses of the drug that made it to the street were stolen stock from pharmaceutical companies or hospitals. Only recently have drug traffickers been able to synthesize the drug in their own labs.

WHAT TO WATCH FOR

Due to the overlap of effects, the signs of ketamine use can be mistaken for those of a variety of other drugs. The only real way to distinguish its use is by actually questioning the user. Some signs that may indicate ketamine use are listed below.

Physical and Behavioral Signs
- Glassy-eyed stare
- Sharp breathing
- Tremors
- Mania
- Exultation
- Disorientation
- Confusion in simple tasks
- Attendance at raves

Paraphernalia
- Pills or white powders
- Rolled up dollar bills or short, cut drinking straws (used for snorting)
- Rave-style clothing or objects

LYSERGIC ACID DIETHYLAMIDE (LSD)

Classification: hallucinogen
Common Names: LSD, acid
Street Names: Sid, Sidney, Uncle Sid, microdot, blotter, blot, windowpane, cartoon acid
Chemical or Brand Name: lysergic acid diethylamide
Medical Use: none
Physical Dependence: none
Psychological Dependence: none
Dose: orally, injected
Effects: illusions, hallucinations, euphoria, paranoia, altered perceptions of time and space
Duration of Effects: 8 to 12 hours
Effects of Overdose: insomnia, elongated trip (drug rush), episodic psychosis (a bad trip), possible long-term or permanent pupil dilation, permanent psychological distress
Withdrawal Symptoms: none
Approximate Cost per Dose: $3 per hit (dose)

FACTS

Lysergic acid diethylamide (LSD) is a synthetically produced hallucinogen. As such, it chemically affects the brain, resulting in behavioral changes, visual and aural hallucinations, impaired depth and time perception. It causes euphoria, and subsequently it eliminates pain sensations. Color, sound and touch are all intertwined for the user, as the drug's effect causes confusion in the brain's interpretation of sensory input. LSD effects generally last around four hours, and are accompanied by an inability to sleep. There are many dangers that accompany LSD use: the regulation of a dose; the danger of bad batches of the drug which can cause very intense and unpleasant effects; irresponsible and dangerous behavior of a user under the influence of LSD; and flashbacks, or vivid reoccurrences of hallucinations when the user is not under the influence. In some instances, permanent psychological distress can result from the use of LSD.

LSD is distributed in a variety of ways. Raw LSD is crystalline, but is cut (diluted) with inert, or non-toxic, agents. It can also be diluted with water and sold as a liquid. LSD is a difficult drug to detect due to the innocuous forms in which it is presented, most often in a tablet known as a microdot. While LSD can be injected, it is most commonly taken orally. Three other common oral forms of the drug are listed below.

- *Sugar cubes* The liquid LSD is poured on a common sugar cube.
- *Gelatin* Liquid LSD can be cut with edible gelatin, set and cut into thin squares called windowpanes for distribution. This form of LSD comes in many different colors, each batch tinted with standard kitchen food coloring.
- *Blotter paper* Sheets of paper are soaked with liquid LSD. These sheets are then cut into small pieces (roughly 1 square inch). Because the paper can have any picture on it, often the street names for this type of LSD are derived from the cartoons, super heroes or other images that are depicted on the blotter paper (e.g., Superman Acid, Yogi Bear Acid).

HISTORY

LSD was originally synthesized in 1938 by Dr. Albert Hoffman as a treatment for hemophilia due to its coagulative properties. Because of its structural similarity to dopamine (a chemical in the brain that acts as a neurotransmitter) and the similarity of its effects to certain aspects of psychosis, LSD was used as a research tool to study and control mental illness. Timothy Leary, Ph.D., a demagogue of the 1960s drug culture, firmly advocated the use of LSD in his "metaprogramming" technique to treat violent psychotics. Leary was able to show some success with the use of LSD in this regard, though his findings are considered dubious by most scholars today.

After an initial popularity as a recreational drug in the 1960s, LSD made a comeback in the 1990s. However, the current average oral dose consumed by users today is 30 to 50 micrograms, a decrease of nearly 90% from the 1960 average dose of 250 to 300 micrograms. Lower potency doses probably account for the relatively few LSD-related emergency incidents during the past several years. The false sense of security derived from this statistic is likely responsible for the drug's present level of popularity among young people.

WHAT TO WATCH FOR

LSD is usually used at parties and in social situations, so be particularly vigilant if your child has been out to a rave, party or other social function. LSD intoxication is difficult to mask. Because the mind's perceptions are warped by the drug, the user will not usually have the wherewithal to recognize that they don't look sober. Some signs that may indicate LSD use are listed below.

Physical and Behavioral Signs
- Dilated pupils
- Wide-eyed stares
- Low body temperature
- Nausea
- Sweat
- Increased blood sugar
- Rapid heart rate
- Unwarranted or inappropriate laughter
- Odd mannerisms (funny faces, erratic movements)
- Sudden bursts of irrational inspirations

Paraphernalia
- Pieces of blotter paper (usually with super hero or cartoon images)
- Psychedelic lamps and lights

MARIJUANA

Classification: depressant
Common Names: marijuana, pot, cannabis
Chemical or Brand Name: n/a (active ingredient: delta-9-tetrahydrocannabinol, or THC)
Street Names: weed, pot, Mary Jane, grass
Medical Use: to treat glaucoma, nausea, tension
Physical Dependence: none
Psychological Dependence: moderate
Dose: smoked, orally
Effects: euphoria, drowsiness, increased appetite
Duration of Effects: 2 to 4 hours
Effects of Overdose: fatigue, paranoia
Withdrawal Symptom: irritability
Cost per Dose: $5 to $7

FACTS

Marijuana is a tobacco-like substance produced by drying the leaves and flowering tops (buds) of the female cannabis plant. As discussed in the Hashish section of this book, the cannabis plant is either male or female. The male plant does not produce the intoxicating substance delta-9-tetrahydrocannabinol (THC) that is associated with the plant name. The male plant is used to make rope, building materials and cloth. The female cannabis plant, however, produces seeds and buds rich in THC, and is the form of the plant from which marijuana and the drug hash are derived. A seedless variant of the female cannabis plant is sinsemilla. It is popular with marijuana users because of the extremely high concentration of THC.

Marijuana is a depressant, similar to hashish: the THC causes a feeling of euphoria in the user, as well as drowsiness and an increase in appetite. The leaves and buds of the female cannabis plant are generally crushed and rolled into a cigarette form called a joint, placed into a hollowed-out cigar and called a blunt, or placed in a pipe or a bong, and smoked. Marijuana can also be added to food and eaten, although this is fairly difficult to do, and thus, relatively uncommon.

Though marijuana is often considered innocuous, especially com-

•••••
Marijuana

pared to heroin and cocaine, there are significant danger issues surrounding its use. While some still laud marijuana use as a healthy alternative to recreational alcohol consumption, the drug contains known toxins and cancer-causing chemicals. Marijuana users are also susceptible to the same health problems as tobacco smokers, including bronchitis, emphysema, pneumonia and asthma. Furthermore, while the pro-legalization factions argue that marijuana is simply a relaxing, social drug, they neglect to mention that marijuana is often laced with any number of adulterants (including PCP) that are designed to increase the effects and toxicity of these products, but which are very dangerous themselves.

Furthermore, marijuana today is much more potent that marijuana of the 1960s and 1970s. In the U.S., marijuana used to be an imported commodity, but hydroponics labs and domestic research into the isolation and intensification of THC has ranked American marijuana among the most potent in the world. For example, the average THC content of sinsemilla produced in the U.S. had risen from 3.2% in 1977 to 12.8% in 1997. A joint no longer produces just a simple high.

AVAILABILITY AND STATISTICS

As a result of the popularity of domestic marijuana, the Drug Enforcement Administration (DEA), the Federal Bureau of Investigation (FBI), and state and regional police forces have been very active in the pursuit of marijuana growers and dealers in the U.S.. For example, the DEA initiated the Domestic Cannabis Eradication and Suppression Program in 1979, which is the only nationwide program to exclusively addresses marijuana. The program began operations in Hawaii and California and rapidly expanded to include all 50 states by 1985.

The labors of the government have resulted in a drastic reduction in illicit sales, but statistics from the DEA reflect a growing tide of illicit activity both domestically and abroad. In 1998, the five leading states for indoor growing activity were California, Florida, Oregon, Alaska, and Kentucky. Nationwide drug law enforcement authorities seize almost 3,000 indoor growing operations annually.

Mexico is responsible for supplying most of the foreign marijuana available in the U.S.. However, drug traffickers based in Southeast Asia countries such as Cambodia and Thailand, also cultivate and ship marijuana to the U.S.. Marijuana from Thailand, or Thai sticks, is seized much less frequently than marijuana originating from Mexico.

The west coast of Canada, specifically the interior of British Columbia, has proven to be a major source of marijuana and hashish. The remote regions, mountainous terrain, and pro-legalization movements in B.C. have allowed a boom in both indoor and outdoor growing operations. Joint task forces from both the Royal Canadian Mounted Police (RCMP) and the DEA regularly net crops in excess of a ton in this region of Canada.

The number of marijuana-related emergency room episodes, which are tracked by the Drug Abuse Warning Network (DAWN), has steadily increased from 15,706 in 1990, to 87,150 in 1999. Many of these visits can be attributed to the fact that the potency of marijuana had also increased during that same period. The 1999 National Household Survey on Drug Abuse (NHSDA) estimated that 5.1% (11.2 million) of the population aged 12 and older were monthly marijuana or hashish users, which is the same rate as in 1991 but considerably lower than the rate of 13.2% in 1979. NHSDA also found that the number of first-time marijuana users in 1998 (2.3 million) increased significantly compared to 1989 (1.4 million). In addition, according to the Office of National Drug Control Policy's 1998 Drug Control Strategy, marijuana is the most prevalent illegal drug in the U.S.: 77% of current illegal drug users used marijuana or hashish in 1996.

In 1999 the NHSDA found that the usage among 12 to 17 year olds nearly doubled from 1992: nearly one in 13 were current users of marijuana. A staggering 50% of 13 year olds reported that they could find and purchase marijuana, and 49% of teens surveyed said they first tried marijuana at age 13 or younger. According to a survey conducted by Phoenix House (a research and drug abuse treatment organization) marijuana was the drug of choice for 87% of teens entering drug treatment programs in New York during the first quarter of 1999.

SPECIAL CONCERNS

Contrary to pro-legalization literature, a Phoenix House survey found that 60% of the youth interviewed affirmed that using marijuana made it easier for them to consume other drugs. Put simply, exposure to the marijuana subculture also exposed these kids to a world of heroin, cocaine and PCP. How does this happen?

There are drug dealers who sell only marijuana. However, it is common for a marijuana dealer to also sell other drugs, particularly PCP

Marijuana

and cocaine. What often occurs is that the dealer will run out of marijuana at a crucial time, say on a Saturday night, when the buyer is supposed to go to a party. Shortages of the drug happen often, either because the dealer has sold all of the supply or because the police have intercepted it. When a shortage happens, a dealer will usually offer a substitute drug— PCP, cocaine, et cetera—at the same price. Faced with this situation, many youths will opt to try the new drug simply because it's there and the marijuana is not. Even though the dealer will initially take a financial loss on the transaction, the buyer will have moved on to a more expensive and addictive drug, which they will most likely buy more of in the future, and the dealer will profit in the long run. This is how so many kids who proclaim that marijuana use is their only vice become involved in heavier drugs. The drug industry is designed to take them from the inexpensive to the expensive drugs.

WHAT TO WATCH FOR

The most obvious sign of marijuana use is the *smell*. Like tobacco smoke, marijuana smoke gets in the clothing and hair of the person smoking it.

Sergeant Marc Pearson of the RCMP gives some simple advice to parents who suspect their child is using marijuana: use your nose. Smell your child's laundry, coats, tote bags—anything they would normally carry around. If they have been involved in marijuana use, there will be the telltale odor similar to that of burning oregano.

Sergeant Pearson also advises parents to look for masked odors. Heavy perfumes, incense, or colognes that your child does not normally use could indicate that they are attempting to cover up the odor of marijuana.

You should also be aware of the many other signs of marijuana use, most notably "roaches". A roach is a small butt of a joint, unlike an unfiltered cigarette butt. It is called a roach because it bears a resemblance to a common cockroach in both color and size. Look for these butts in ashtrays, behind a shed or other remote place around the home or in a small jar in the child's room. Because of the high THC content in roaches, they are sometimes saved for use when the user has no other marijuana source. Some other signs that may indicate marijuana use are listed below.

Physical and Behavioral Signs
- Dilated pupils
- Red or bloodshot eyes
- Respiratory problems
- Apathy
- Dreaminess, euphoria
- Unwarranted or excessive laughter
- Increased appetite
- Paranoia
- Strange or masked odors

Paraphernalia
- Incense, air fresheners
- Pipes, bongs (a bong is an elaborate pipe, essentially a water filled bowl with a hose)
- Joints, blunts, "roaches", rolling papers and cigarette rolling equipment
- Roach clips (small tweezers-like tools used to hold and smoke "roaches")
- Eye drops (to mask red eyes)
- Bags of herbal substances
- Pro-cannabis literature, stickers, patches, posters, et cetera

MDMA (ECSTASY)

Classification: stimulant (synthetic psychoactive stimulant)
Common Names: ecstasy, MDMA
Street Names: E, ecstasy or XTC
Chemical or Brand Name: 3, 4-methylenedioxymethamphetamine
Medical Use: none (MDMA was originally used in psychotherapy)
Physical Dependence: none
Psychological Dependence: moderate
Dose: orally
Effects: hallucination, euphoria, paranoia
Duration of Effects: 4 to 6 hours
Effects of Overdose: nausea, hallucinations, chills, sweating, increased body temperature, tremors, involuntary teeth clenching, muscle cramping, blurred vision
Withdrawal Symptoms: anxiety, hallucination, depression
Approximate Cost per Dose: $20 to $30

FACTS

MDMA, or ecstasy as it is more commonly known, is a hallucinogen and a stimulant. It is a synthetic, or "designer", drug and an amphetamine derivative. Like ketamine, MDMA is often referred to as a "club drug": it is used frequently at raves and other forms of club entertainment events because of the stimulant-hallucinogen crossover effect. Essentially, MDMA is a cross between an amphetamine or methamphetamine, and the hallucinogen mescaline. It was first synthesized as an appetite suppressant in 1912 by a German company. It is a chemical analog of methylenedioxyamphetamine (MDA), a synthetic hallucinogenic drug that was popular in the 1960s. Until the late 1980s and early 1990s, MDMA was primarily used illicitly as an additive to other drugs, notably cannabis, but now it is common for MDMA to be taken orally as a pill or tablet. Proponents of the drug allege that it creates a profound and positive feeling for life characterized by empathy for others, elimination of anxiety, a relaxed mood, and it can cause an increase in sex drive. Because of its original design as a diet drug, MDMA also suppresses the need to eat, drink, or sleep, enabling users to endure parties that may last for several days. For this reason, its use can lead to severe dehydration or exhaustion, and thus MDMA users pay constant attention to their fluid levels (hence the tradition of providing free orange juice to all participants at raves). The drug is also popular in other counterculture scenes, namely, among "goths" (short for "gothic", meaning a lifestyle and fashion sense characterized by black clothing and pale face-makeup) and punks.

While MDMA is not as addictive as heroin or cocaine, prolonged use of the drug can be as physically devastating as an overdose. Signs of prolonged use are nausea, hallucinations, chills, sweating, increased body temperature, tremors, involuntary teeth clenching, muscle cramping, and blurred vision. An MDMA overdose is characterized by high blood pressure, faintness and panic attacks. More severe cases of MDMA overdose can result in loss of consciousness, seizures and a drastic rise in body temperature that can cause extreme heat stroke or heart failure. Studies performed on long-term MDMA users show damage to the neurons in the brain that transmit serotonin, an important biochemical involved in a variety of critical functions including learning, sleep and integration of emotion. Even recreational MDMA users are at risk of developing permanent brain damage that may manifest as depression, anxiety, memory loss and other neuropsychotic disorders.

AVAILABILITY AND STATISTICS

MDMA is primarily an imported drug with almost no domestic production. The MDMA distributed in North America is usually synthesized in labs in Western Europe, primarily the Netherlands and Belgium. According to the Drug Enforcement Administration (DEA), Israeli organized crime syndicates, some associated with Russian organized crime syndicates, have forged relationships with Western European MDMA traffickers and gained control over a significant share of the European market. The Israeli syndicates are currently the primary source for U.S. distribution groups of the drug.

In the U.S., MDMA is sold in bulk quantity at the mid-wholesale level for approximately $8 per dose. The retail price of MDMA sold on the street remains steady at $20 to $30 per dose. In marketing the drug, dealers use brand names and logos that coincide with holidays or special events. Among the more popular images are

MDMA
Ecstasy

butterflies, lightning bolts, and four-leaf clovers.

MDMA use results in a large number of drug-related hospital visits, due to the dehydration and exhaustion that often accompanies MDMA use, as well as the volatile nature of the drug. The Drug Abuse Warning Network's (DAWN) estimates reveal that nationwide hospital emergency room reports of MDMA incidents rose from 70 in 1993 to 2,850 in 1999. There have also been drastic increases of police seizures of MDMA: according to the DEA's statistics, seizures of MDMA tablets submitted to their laboratories have risen from a total of 196 in 1993 to 143,600 in 1998, while seizures from January through May 1999 total over 216,300 tablets of the drug.

SPECIAL CONCERNS

MDMA is not used when drinking because the chemical functions of the drug inhibit or neutralize the effects of alcohol in the system. For this reason, many of the alcohol-free "teen dance clubs" are in fact havens for MDMA use. Because parents feel safe about the alcohol-free environment, they will let their kids go to these types of teen dance clubs. However, drug dealers and users take this opportunity to introduce and encourage MDMA as an alternative to alcohol. Parents should be aware that both raves and alcohol-free nightclubs foster MDMA use, even though the owners and proprietors of these establishments don't necessarily encourage this kind of illicit activity.

WHAT TO WATCH FOR

Because MDMA is a club, or party, drug, its use at home is virtually non-existent. Discovering if your child is using MDMA is difficult, and can only be ascertained by virtue of the clues. Some signs that may indicate MDMA use are listed below.

Physical and Behavioral Signs
- Feverish with no other symptoms of illness
- Drastic weight loss
- Blissful and exuberant when returning from a party; miserable and depressed several hours later
- Long absences from home
- Attendance at raves

Paraphernalia
- Baby pacifiers and other rave-related objects
- Evidence of rave or alcohol-free dance club attendance

•••••
MDMA
Ecstasy

PEYOTE MESCALINE (MESCALINE)

Classification: hallucinogen
Common Names: peyote, mescaline
Street Names: mescal, buttons, cat tie, cactus juice, mesc
Chemical or Brand Name: n/a
Medical Use: none
Physical Dependence: none
Psychological Dependence: none
Dose: orally
Effects: illusions and hallucinations, altered perceptions of time and space
Duration of Effects: 8 to 12 hours, depending on metabolism
Effects of Overdose: long and intense trip (drug rush) episodes, psychosis
Withdrawal Symptoms: none
Approximate Cost per Dose: $20

FACTS

Peyote mescaline, or simply mescaline, is a naturally occurring hallucinogenic drug. Peyote is a small, spineless cactus native to Mexico. Mescaline is a strong hallucinogen that occurs naturally in the button-like tops of the peyote cactus, and is thus the active ingredient in peyote mescaline. When dried, the cactus tops are called buttons, or crowns. A dose of mescaline is about 0.3 to 0.5 grams contained in roughly 5 grams of dried peyote buttons. While mescaline occurs naturally in other southwest-American plants, the most common way of taking the drug is in the form of the peyote button.

There is no doubt that peyote mescaline produces some of the most intense and dramatic hallucinogenic effects known. The mescaline induced euphoria, or trip, is an other-worldly experience full of sexual and mystical imagery. While the user is generally aware they are experiencing illusions, they are often overwhelmed by the vivid intensity of the hallucinations nonetheless, and are struck with a sense of awe and wonderment. These effects can last for up to 12 hours, roughly twice as long as the average LSD trip.

Peyote mescaline is consumed orally, by eating the buttons. They are chewed for 10 to 20 minutes, allowing the saliva to break down the husk of the button so that the mescaline can enter the user's system. The immediate effect of mescaline is vomiting: the body recognizes the poisonous elements of the drug and reacts by trying to purge itself. However, enough of the mescaline is absorbed prior to the purging reaction for the hallucinogenic effect to occur.

The main hazard of mescaline is not the drug's effect on the body, rather it is the state of mind that it produces in the user. While intoxicated, a user is so absorbed by the hallucinations that they are almost totally oblivious to their environment; thus, they are completely vulnerable to their surroundings and circumstances. As with the drug GHB, individuals who are under the influence of peyote mescaline can not only harm themselves by falling into dangerous situations, but they can be harmed by others, possibly being raped, robbed or brutalized. In their intoxicated state, the user will have no knowledge of what is happening to them, and when they are sober, they will have no recollection.

• • • • •
Peyote Mescaline

HISTORY

The use of peyote mescaline as a hallucinogen originates with the Native American tribes, long before European settlers arrived in North America. The drug was strictly used in a religious context: the mescaline trip was a rite of passage for the shaman, not a pastime for all Native Americans. The inherent dangers of mescaline use were well known to the Native Americans, and safeguards were established to prevent its abuse.

Mescaline came into popular use in the 1960s, and has remained ever since. It was made fashionable by artists and musicians such as Jim Morrison of the rock group the Doors whose lyrics and poetry expounded on the mystical aspect of the peyote high. Today, the use of mescaline as a religious ritual is often cited as a justification for its use as a recreational drug. However, it is important to recognize that the Native Americans monitored and restricted mescaline use in their culture almost as stringently the Drug Enforcement Administration (DEA) does today.

SPECIAL CONCERNS

If you suspect your child has taken mescaline, it is highly recommended that medical attention be sought due to the severity of the

Peyote Mescaline

symptoms. While there are no standard treatments for mescaline intoxication, a medical professional is best suited to deal with the situation. The chance always exists that your child is not on mescaline and that their symptoms stem from a legitimate medical condition. It is generally proscribed that the user be isolated and monitored in an intensive care unit until the high has passed, but this decision would be up to your doctor.

WHAT TO WATCH FOR

Mescaline use is very difficult to hide. The high it produces incapacitates the user to such a degree that any parent should readily be able to recognize that something is amiss. Some signs that may indicate mescaline use are listed below.

Physical and Behavioral Signs
- Vomiting
- Wide-eyes stares
- Talking to oneself
- Mania
- Volatile emotional swings characterized by weeping, broad smiles and anguished cries

Paraphernalia
- Small, round brown or black disks (peyote mescaline buttons)

PHENCYCLIDINE (PCP)

Classification: hallucinogen
Common Name: PCP
Street Names: angel dust, PCP, hog, TCP, powder puff
Chemical or Brand Name: phencyclidine
Medical Use: none (PCP was once used as an anesthetic)
Physical Dependence: none
Psychological Dependence: extremely high
Dose: smoked, snorted, injected
Effects: illusions and hallucinations, altered perception of time and space
Duration of Effects: 3 to 4 hours
Effects of Overdose: long and intense trip (drug rush) episodes, psychosis, possible death
Withdrawal Symptoms: none
Approximate Cost per Dose: $20

FACTS

Phencyclidine (PCP) is a synthetically produced hallucinogen. It produces a wide array of effects, ranging from numbness and detachment, to visual and aural hallucinations, to anxiety and paranoia. It may result in violent behavior and psychosis which appears similar to schizophrenia. PCP is most commonly sold on the street under the names angel dust, killer weed, embalming fluid, and rocket fuel.

Pure PCP is white powder that looks similar to cocaine or baking soda. It is distributed as a powder or a liquid. The powder is usually cut (diluted) with another substance, thus altering the color from white to brown. This dilution not only affects the price and quality of the drug, but, as with any cut drug, it can result in some very bad reactions in the user. The powder is generally snorted, or can be smoked. To get liquid PCP, the powder is dissolved in the highly flammable chemical ether. The liquid PCP can either be injected, but it is more commonly sprayed onto marijuana or another leafy substance and smoked in a joint or cigarette.

The chemicals needed to synthesize PCP are easy to obtain and

PCP

inexpensive. Because PCP is easy to create, requiring little chemical knowledge or equipment, illicit labs can be set up and maintained by the most inexperienced of dealers. As a result, PCP is often sold in urban neighborhoods by small-time dealers looking to a quick buck by lacing their marijuana with PCP to heighten the effects.

PCP is a dangerous drug not only because of the intense, unpredictable and harmful effects it produces, but because it is undetectable when it is added to relatively mild drugs such as marijuana. Generally, the user will only know that their marijuana was laced with PCP after the fact, when it is too late. (This is yet another reason why marijuana use should not be thought of as a simple, herbal alternative to alcohol.)

HISTORY

PCP was originally used as an anesthetic in the 1950s, but was discontinued when the medical professionals discovered that the side effects were too grievous to condone. PCP became commercially available for use as a veterinary anesthetic in the 1960s under the trade name of Sernylan, but was later banned from use in veterinary clinics due to a growing abuse of the drug in popular culture. At present there is no legal medical use for PCP and no pharmaceutical company makes the drug. All PCP available in North America today is made in illegal labs.

WHAT TO WATCH FOR

PCP effects vary depending on potency and cut. Some signs that may indicate PCP use are listed below.

Physical and Behavioral Signs
- Slurred speech
- Rapid or involuntary eye movements
- Lack of coordination
- Staggered walk
- Talking to oneself (auditory or visual hallucination)
- A numbness of the extremities, moving up to the face and head
- Paranoia and anxiety
- Severe mood swings
- Violent hostility; a sense of strength or power

Paraphernalia
- Marijuana or bags of ground herbs
- Track marks (needle marks and bruises on the arms from repeated injections)

•••••
PCP

CONVERSATION WITH A DRUG DEALER

Conversation with a dealer

The drug dealer is the one person who would be most responsible for exposing your child to a wide variety of illicit substances. They are also the person who you will never hear from when you are discussing drug abuse with your child. For this reason, I interviewed several drug dealers to find out more about the business of drugs. What follows is one of the more enlightening discussions I had during my research.

How does one become a dealer, and why?
You don't become a dealer. It's not like being a doctor or a lawyer. It's something you usually just wind up doing so you can pay for the stuff you want. I mean, rich kids don't become dealers because they can afford the drugs they want. If you don't have Mommy's and Daddy's money to blow on pot when they're not looking, you have to find other ways of getting it. One of the best ways to do that is to sell.

How much money do you make?
Money? No one makes money at this. At least not the guys actually selling it. And most of the guys you see on the street actually dealing make absolutely nothing. The whole idea of the rich drug dealer is just a myth. I've been in this business for ten years and I've yet to meet a single person who could pay their rent with what they make off drugs. The higher ups, the guys that actually import the stuff, yeah, they make money. But it's a pyramid scheme, you know? The guys at the bottom get shafted while the guys at the top who don't actually do any of the work get all the profits.

Then why do it?
It pays the bills—the ones I'm worried about, anyway. I mean, welfare covers the rent, barely. I suppose I make enough to get the odd groceries, but I have to watch that. I mean, you think you're doing well, and then three weeks into the month you figure out you've spent all the money you've made, and you still owe the guy who fronts you the stuff, so you're screwed. Or, sometimes you get ripped off, that happens a lot.

Who rips you off?
People. Guys. They find out where you're dealing from if you're not careful, and, sooner or later, a bunch of them will show up with baseball bats and clean you out.

Has this happened to you?
It happens all the time—well, not all the time. It's happened to me twice in the last year or so, anyway. But it always leaves you screwed. It takes months to make it up, and in the meantime you've got to live on nothing. You wind up using your rent money to pay off "the guys upstairs", just so they don't come and kick the hell out of you for getting robbed. They don't cut you any slack, and they don't care if you've gotten ripped off. They just want their cash when you said you'd pay them. It's business.

•••••
Conversation with a dealer

You sell to a lot of students, right?
I sell to a lot of everybody, but students, yeah. They come by a lot. They get to know where I'm at.

So you have no problem selling to kids? What's the youngest age you'd sell to, or is there a limit?
Look, it's not like I'm all in favor of little kids getting stoned—I'm not. I've said no to a lot of kids. The older ones—twelfth grade or something—I'll sell to them. The younger ones aren't good for business—people hear about you dealing to 12 year olds and you get a bad reputation.

So where do the younger ones get the drugs if not from guys like you?
Usually from the other kids at school. You know, someone's older brother comes in here, buys four grams of pot for ten bucks a gram. He turns around and sells two grams to his kid brother and his friends for, like, 20 bucks a gram and he winds up making all his money back—or something like that. Everyone's trying to get away without having to pay for the stuff, you know?

What would you tell parents who are trying to keep their kids off drugs?
The first thing I'd tell them is that it's not my problem. I'm fed up with people that look at dealers and think how evil and horrible we are. I provide products, that's what I do. If your kid wants them he'll

Conversation with a dealer

get them, through me or someone else. And every time some kid ODs or flips out, everyone in the world wants to punish the dealers. If the same kid had gotten his hands on a bottle of booze, do you think anybody's going to show up at the liquor store and start screaming at the guy behind the counter? It's not going to happen—not like it would to a dealer, anyway. But because I sell the stuff that's not government sanctioned, I get the flack. With any legal drug sold over the counter the blame would be where it's supposed to be: on the kid that wanted to do the stuff in the first place.

What do you say to people who accuse you of manipulating high school kids into using heavier drugs?
You mean, like getting the kids hooked on crystal meth or something? No one gets you hooked on anything. I've seen a lot of people, kids and adults, doing a lot of different drugs. Some of them, most of them, are able to do their trip, come down and go home, no problem. But there's always that one person: you can see it in their eyes when they're stoned, and you know this one's not going to walk away because he likes it too much.

But you make more money from the PCP and meth than the pot, right?
Well, yeah. And I'm not going to tell you that I would rather have them buying pot than meth, because I wouldn't. But you have to understand, you read all the stuff about addiction and deaths related to stuff like PCP and it gets scary. Me? I've never seen an OD of PCP happen, and I've sold hundreds of hits. Meth? Yeah, I've seen kids get real whacked on it for a long time, but they usually grow out of it. Although, I know of one girl that died on meth. But any dealer will tell you that you have to come clean [detoxify] from meth or it's not worth doing: too much and you don't even get high anymore. It's just money down the toilet.

How do parents stop their kids from winding up here in your apartment buying drugs from you?
That part's easy. It's the same with every dealer, everywhere. No one gets through my door unless I know who they are. It's just too easy to get busted. If someone wants to get in here, they have to be brought in by someone I know and trust. You're never going to find a dealer that'll let anybody walk into his place and just start buying stuff—it

just doesn't happen. If a parent really wants to keep their kid out of here, I'd tell them to make sure their kid isn't hanging around with someone who comes here. Plain and simple. If a kid tried knocking on my door and I didn't know him, I'd scare the hell out of him and make sure he never came back.

Anything else?
Yeah—clothes, I suppose. A kid shows up here looking like Beaver Cleaver, and he won't be welcome. I mean, even if he were brought in by someone I know, the straight look puts off customers. No one wants to walk in here and see a kid dressed like he just stepped out of Sunday school. That kid would probably get his head kicked in, and not by me.

●●●●●
Conversation with a dealer

Why do you figure the police are unable to stop dealers from dealing drugs?
(Laughter) You're kidding me, right? Cops do stop dealers. It happens all the time. Pretty much every dealer's been busted at least once. Hell, it's easy to get busted. You kind of accept it as part of the job. But there are ways to avoid it, or at least delay it.

First thing is, you never deal on the street. If you go out, you don't take anything for sale with you—that's just stupid. You make friends in the right social circles, and you let them know where you are and have them come to you.

Second, if anyone comes by who you don't know, they don't get in. It's a lot harder for a cop to harass you if it's in your own home instead of on the street. On the street, the cops can say you were doing something wrong and use that as a reason to search you; but in your own home, they need a warrant or a damn good reason for coming in.

Third, you keep moving. Don't deal out of the same apartment for too long or word gets around and the cops find a reason to come in and bust you. If you keep moving every four to six months, they never have enough time to catch up with you.

PREVENTION

Even though drugs are such a large part of popular culture today, there are ways that a parent can take action when it comes to drug use and their child. The first and best way to combat drugs in your home is to prevent drug use. Unfortunately, sometimes prevention is not enough. Parents should also be aware of how to confront drug use if your child should become involved with an illicit substance. The next two chapters will give you some of the information you need to know about prevention and confrontation so that you can begin to take action against the the drugs of today.

WHAT A PARENT CAN DO
While no family is immune to the influence of the drug culture, a parent can strive to ensure that their child has the support and confidence they need to refrain from drug use. There are several things a parent can do to help prevent drug use: know your child, set an example, discuss your values and establish and enforce rules.

KNOW YOUR CHILD
The National Center on Addiction and Substance Abuse (NCASA) offers some excellent advice to parents who are striving to keep their children safe. All of the reasons center around one key idea: your best defense is to know your child. The best way to do this is to spend time and talk with them.

- Become an active participant in your child's life.
- Help your child with their homework regularly.
- Encourage your child to seek your help on important decisions.
- Eat dinners as a family frequently.
- Attend social or religious activities regularly, and make them an important part of your child's life.
- Watch for reasons to praise your child, and follow through when they've done well.
- Know where your child is after school and on weekends, and what they are doing.

SET AN EXAMPLE
The Drug Enforcement Administration (DEA), the Drug Abuse Resistance Education (DARE) program and The National Center on Addiction and Substance Abuse (NCASA) all agree on how best to deal with suspected child drug abuse. These agencies acknowledge that every family is unique and every parent struggles with the individual needs and expectations of their child. They do, however, stress it is important for a parent to realize that their child is always learning from them, even in the most heated argument.

When your child was young, they would follow you around, and pretend to be just like you. If you were cleaning, they'd pick up a toy broom and pretend to sweep. If you were on the phone, they would be on their toy phone. They were always trying to mimic your behaviors. Of course, as children grow into young adults, they rebel. But even when rebelling, they are still watching and taking their cues from their parents. Believe it or not, your child will mimic your values in the school yard, when faced with peer pressure or drugs, just as they copied your actions as a toddler. All drug counseling services share the same message in this regard.

As parents, it is necessary that you demonstrate your value system in the home, especially when it comes to drug use. Annabel Williams of the Prevention Awareness for Life Program explained in an interview for this book that children who decide not to abuse alcohol or drugs usually do so because they have preconceived ideas about drug use and abuse. Long before a teacher or school counselor comes into the classrooms to teach them to "Just Say No" most kids have already decided whether drugs are for them or not. Williams explains that these decisions are based on the values and ideas they've learned at home. A parent must be explicit when discussing drugs because any ambiguity on the part of the parent can readily be interpreted either as not caring (in which case the decision is left up to the child in the face of peer pressure) or as condoning the drug use by not speaking out against it.

DISCUSS YOUR VALUES
The National Clearinghouse for Alcohol and Drug Information offers some helpful advice to parents who want to ensure that their values are clearly conveyed to their children.

Prevention

1. *Communicate Your Values Openly* Discuss why values such as honesty, self-reliance and responsibility are important, how they help people make good decisions. Teach your child that good decisions accumulate to build a strong, positive character, and that being in the habit of making good choices makes decision making easier.

2. *Discuss Values Regularly* Make sure your child understands your family values. It is important to reinforce the values you have discussed: it helps to bring out any issues your child does not understand, and it helps them to incorporate these beliefs into their life. You can test your child's understanding by discussing some common situations at the dinner table: for example, you could discuss a question like, "What would you do if a person ahead of you in line at the theater dropped a five-dollar bill?"

3. *Teach by Example* Recognize how your actions affect the development of your child's values. It is argued that children whose parents smoke, for example, are more likely to become smokers. Evaluate your own use of tobacco, alcohol, prescription medication and even over-the-counter drugs. Consider how your attitudes and actions may be shaping your child's choices about alcohol and drug use.

Of course, if you are in the habit of having wine with dinner, an occasional beer or cocktail, you don't necessarily have to stop, just make sure you discuss it with your child. Children can understand and accept that there are differences between what adults may do legally and what is appropriate and legal for children. However, it is advisable to keep the distinction sharp: don't let your children become involved in your drinking by mixing a cocktail for you or bringing you a beer, and don't allow your child to have sips of your drink.

4. *Do What You Say, Say What You Do* Look for conflicts between your words and your actions. Remember that children learn by example. Telling your child to say that you are not at home because a phone call comes at an inconvenient time is, in effect, teaching your child that it is all right to be dishonest. Children are quick to pick up on these types of contradictory signals.

ESTABLISH AND ENFORCE RULES

There is no doubt that teenagers test the limits of their parents' permissiveness. Most will try to get away with things they know you would not normally permit. While this phase is a normal part of maturation, it can be a hellish experience for the parent.

DARE acknowledges that it can be difficult for parents to be tough disciplinarians all the time: they love their child and want to see them happy, yet they must "be the bad guy" and enforce the rules. During the often rough years of raising a teenager, many parents begin to feel that the warmth and love in the parent-child relationship becomes overwhelmed by the constant questioning, arguments and disciplinary measures. Too often upholding the "right" decisions can leave a parent feeling like the tyrannical ogre their child may accuse them of being. DARE and the Prevention Awareness for Life Program suggest one way to smooth out this kind of rough relationship: explain your reasons for your rules and decisions, and make sure your child understands that they are rooted in love and concern for their health and happiness.

When it comes to setting limits, there is room to discuss the rules and possibly negotiate. However, when it comes to issues like drug abuse, a parent must remember that they must set firm, non-negotiable limits. It is, quite literally, about keeping your child alive.

1. Know What You're Talking About Before you set the limits about drug use, Annabel Williams of the Prevention Awareness for Life Program provides a good tip. She advises parents to become as literate and knowledgeable of available drugs as their children are. Because your child will probably have heard of most street drugs, your best defense is to know more than they do. Police and counseling centers agree that if the parent doesn't have enough information, or if they have misinformation about street drugs, the child will likely dismiss what the parent says as misinformed hype. However, children will likely know only street-level information on street drugs: the names, the high they produce, et cetera. If you are aware of the different effects each kind of drug produces, and can further inform your child of the dangers of each, you will be taken seriously.

Furthermore, let your child know that you're familiar with the street names and effects of drugs, as well as the paraphernalia associated with each. Your child will be far more likely to stay clear of drugs

• • • •
Rules

and drug paraphernalia for fear of ready detection by an informed parent.

2. Set the Limits Again, health care professionals are in full agreement about the standards of discipline where drug use is suspected or evident. According to DARE, the key to discipline is consistency. Make sure that you are consistent in setting, explaining and enforcing the rules. Listed below is what the DARE web site suggests for setting and enforcing rules.

• • • • •
Rules

- *Set the Rules* Be specific, tell your child what the rules are and what behavior is expected. Make it clear to your child that a no-alcohol, no-drug-use rule remains the same at all times—in your home, in a friend's home, anywhere your child goes. Discuss the specific consequences for breaking the rules.
- *Explain Why* Explain the rules and the reasons for the rules. Don't lie or exaggerate the truth about drugs: kids know the drug scene as well or better than you. Your best defense is to explain to them in detail what these drugs do. Use the reference from this book for details, or log on to the DEA web site and download the most current details about illicit drugs and their effects. Present these to your child for discussion.
- *Enforce the Rules* Follow through with the limits you've set. Never, ever allow your child to circumvent a punishment that was clearly prescribed before the infraction. To do so allows your child to believe that their behavior really wasn't "that bad" and that you're really not that upset about it all. When a rule is broken, don't make up a new consequence that was not discussed when you originally set the limits. Avoid overreactions: threats such as "Just wait until your father gets home" or "You're going to get it when your mother hears about this" will only inflame the situation. Instead, react calmly and carry out the punishment that the child expects to receive for breaking the rules.

CONFRONTING DRUG ABUSE

Unfortunately, sometimes, no matter what preventative measures were taken, a child will fall into the world of drugs. In such a situation, a parent hopes that they can address and rectify the problem, before it is too late.

THE INITIAL REACTION

Often, the first inclination a parent has when their child finally comes home at three in the morning after partying is to punish them. It's natural. It's expected. It's also wrong.

A parent's initial reaction to a possible drug use situation is critical. It can shape the outcome of the confrontation to a large degree. It must be handled with care, thought and control. It's important that you not confront your child while they are under the influence of drugs or alcohol. As the Street-Wise web site states, it is important to be fully prepared and ready for confrontation. Your first step should be to control your emotions. If you can refrain from reacting out of anger, fear or hurt, you'll have helped the crisis state to pass and set the stage for a more composed and controlled confrontation. Drug counseling centers suggest that your next step should be to control the situation as best you can, in order to ensure the health and safety of your child.

1. Control Your Emotions The DARE handbook warns against rash behavior or lashing out in anger at your child in a possible drug use situation. It stresses the importance of controlling your own emotional responses so that you may keep a cool head and do what is best for your child: you must remember your role as a parent.

The National Household Survey on Drug Abuse (NHSDA) suggests one way of controlling your emotional response: remember that the child you're waiting for is the same child you cared for as an infant. If you think back to when your child was first born, you'll recall the late-night feedings and diaper changes. When you got up in the middle of the night to change a diaper, you may have grumbled as you went down the hall or complained to a friend about your lack of sleep. But you didn't take it out on the child. Why? Because you instinctively knew that for all the troubles the baby may cause you, it is worth it because you love this child. These facts are just as true for your child as a teenager.

This imagery can help to give you the strength you will need to control your response if you're forced to sit up late at night waiting for your child to come home. As tiresome as these nights can be, they are a lot of what parenting is about. It is an investment you make in your child so you can see that they grow strong and happy, even in the face of their own mistakes. It may not always seem like it, but the rewards of nights like these are always there waiting for you. Any child, no matter the level of their involvement in drugs, is still capable of coming clean and becoming a successful, healthy adult. When they do, you'll be proud and you'll have forgotten about the nights you spent waiting up for them when they were teens.

2. Control the Situation The first rule in confronting drug abuse is to know where and when to confront. When your child walks through the door, and you have your emotions under control, take control of the situation. The priority must be on the health of the child, not on the confrontation. An assessment of the situation is recommended before you take any action. Annabel Williams suggests the parent use their knowledge of their child to decide as best they can whether medical attention is warranted. (Note: if there are any doubts, err on the side of caution. While a trip to the hospital could be for nothing, it is better to get a doctor's opinion if you have the slightest concern about overdose or chemical addiction.) Where no overdose or chemical addiction is present, many physicians and counselors recommend offering the child orange juice, a good idea no matter what drug the child is on. It generally can't hurt and it can help in cases of dehydration and/or malnutrition.

If you are convinced there is no immediate crisis, send your child off to bed. They may or may not go to sleep, so be alert to any sounds, as they may be wandering about in the night. It is a good idea to check on them during the night to make sure they're okay, and to be available if they want to talk to you.

HOW TO CONFRONT YOUR CHILD

When you've examined all the evidence and come to a firm conclusion that your child is, in fact, involved in drug use, your first reaction should be patience. You only get one first-shot at discussing drug abuse with your child, and the way in which you address it will set the tone for all the conversations to follow. While it is imperative that a confrontation occur, it is equally important that it happens in a controlled, organized and planned manner or it could blow up in your face. Again, one should turn to the professionals for the best advice on how to do this. I highly recommend visiting the Street-Wise web site at *home.earthlink.net/~nodrugs/confront.htm*. Their advice is detailed and well written and represents a common-sense approach based in experience. When confronting a drug user, you should prepare for the confrontation, confront the user and then follow up on the confrontation.

•••••
Confronting drug abuse

1. Prepare for the Confrontation Some of the advice Street-Wise offers for parents confronting their children is listed below.

- Don't confront alone. Talk to friends, family, and health care professionals. Have them present when addressing the issues.
- Make sure that the people who are there to assist you in confronting the child are people they will respect (e.g., friends, family members, or a favorite school teacher).
- Set a definite time and date with the assisting parties for an initial meeting without your child to determine if confrontation is warranted. Listen to the advice and information you are given from the people who know your child, and weigh the observations they present honestly. Don't respond to any criticism of your child with offense or hurt.
- Make sure your child has access to assistance 24 hours a day. This will come in handy after the confrontation has taken place, when the child will need support. Solicit the people you are meeting with to be available when you are not, and make sure your child has their contact information.

Set a time and date for the confrontation to occur. Once you have assembled everyone who will be there to assist you, find a neutral place, such as your home, to confront your child. The Prevention Awareness Handbook recommends that you take several steps to set the tone.

Confronting drug abuse

- Make sure your seats are positioned close enough that you and your child can touch hands if necessary, but far enough apart that you can both remain in your own spaces.
- Ensure that your child has no toys, pens or trinkets in their hands that they can play with or use to distract themselves from the discussion.
- Ensure that you will not be disturbed by friends or visitors. Turn the ringer off on the phone or have a third party in the house to deal with unexpected visitors and calls.

2. The Confrontation When everything is in order and your child has arrived, begin by telling the child why they are there, and begin the discussion. The DARE program and Street-Wise outline some points that should be covered when confronting your child.

- Outline the penalties for drug use that you have established beforehand in a clear and concise way, using definite words such as "you will be grounded for five weeks with no allowance". Do not allow any negotiation, complaints or a arguments. If your child complains or tries to offer an excuse, simply carry on with the conversation. Let them understand that the punishment is the least of the worries being addressed here.

- Ask what drug they were on. If they deny usage, refer to the signs you have witnessed and any other evidence you have found. Challenge them to explain it. If they maintain they were not using, tell them that you are willing to take them to the doctor immediately for testing (cite the names the various tests that could be administered). If they maintain innocence, follow through. Have them tested.

- Evaluate their answer. If they tell you what drug was involved, evaluate the signs you witnessed while they were under the influence and compare this to what you know of the drug. Decide if they are telling you the truth. Keep in mind that when confronted, almost every teenager will say they were just trying pot regardless of what drug they were using. They assume that their parents will consider smoking pot to be a minor indiscretion, and thus, they will be let off the hook. Even if they were just using marijuana, there are substantial dangers to this drug use that must be addressed. If your child is lying about the drug involved, explain to them why you don't think they were using that drug and ask them if they can explain why the signs don't coincide.

- Assess the extent of use. Once you establish which drug they were using, ask how long they've been doing it, and with whom. Decide if professional help is needed.

- Sign a contract. While there are many approaches counselors recommend to eliminate drug use from your child's life, Street-Wise suggests that you initiate a clearly worded written contract with your child, outlining in great detail the responsibilities of all concerned parties, and the penalties for violating the contract. (Their web site has several excellent samples of these contracts.) Be aware that your child will probably offer many excuses for their misbehavior. They could assert something like they didn't knowingly take the drug, that someone had slipped it into their drink. If this excuse is given, explain that your intent here is not to "punish" the child but to protect them. Whether the incident happened because the child deliberately took drugs or because their friends duped them, the situation as it stands demonstrates that your child needs protection. Stress that the contract is designed to eliminate drug use. If it was not their fault then the contract will be easy for them to abide by.

AFTERWARDS

In most cases, drug abuse is not an isolated incident. There is a chance that your child may indeed have just been "trying pot for the first time" or that "someone slipped something" in their drink. Even though this would be great to believe, a parent cannot assume this to be the case. Given the statistics of drug use and availability in North American schools, you must interpret this one incident as a part of a trend.

If you know or suspect that your child has developed a pattern of drug use or an addiction, you will probably need to seek professional help. Your first step should be to take your child to your family doc-

Confronting drug abuse

tor. If you don't have one, a local hospital will suffice. Have the doctor examine your child fully for signs of drug abuse, then ask for a reference to a state or local substance abuse agency or county mental health society. Your school district should have a substance abuse coordinator or counselor who can refer you to treatment programs.

Though support, discipline and counseling can certainly help, you have to be prepared for the fact that another drug abuse situation may happen again, especially if your child is dealing with an addiction. But you would not be alone. Parents from every city, state and province in North America are trying to come to grips with the problems and fears associated with child drug abuse. Dozens of societies, groups and associations have been created by people coping with child drug abuse issues in order to provide help, insight and tools to deal with situations similar to theirs. You could contact one of these groups for support. The back of this book provides a list of such groups. You can contact any one of them, or pay attention to the Coming Events section in your local newspaper for times and dates of meetings scheduled in you area.

A FINAL NOTE

Remember, it is your child that you are working for. Although the threat of drug abuse is real, the one overwhelming factor that sways the balance in your child's favor is you, the parent. As a care giver, disciplinarian and role model you will mean more to your child than the influences of peer pressure and pop culture combined.

No matter what ordeal you face, keep loving them, keep trying for them, and put up with being the "bad guy" for as long as it takes. As with the other trials you've seen your child through, this too shall pass. If you ever doubt this, it may help to keep this quote in mind

When I was 17 my parents were the stupidest people I knew. When I turned 20 I was amazed at how much they'd learned in only three years.
—Roy Rogers

GLOSSARY OF DRUG SLANG, JARGON AND STREET TERMS

The following is a sample of the key terms listed on the Metrich web site at *www.metrich.com/slang/slang.htm*. It is a brief list of key drug terms your child may have picked up at school or through friends. By knowing and understanding these terms, you'll find it far easier to detect what drugs your child may be involved in.

● ● ● ● ●
Drug slang & street terms

5 MINUTE PSYCHOSIS – dimethyltryptamine

ACAPULCO GOLD – marijuana from southwestern Mexico

ACAPULCO RED – marijuana

ACE – marijuana; PCP

ACID – LSD

ACID HEAD – an LSD user

AD – PCP

ADAM – MDMA

AFRICAN BLACK – marijuana

AFRICAN BUSH – marijuana

AIMIES – amphetamines

ALICE – LSD

ALL LIT UP – to be under the influence of drugs

AMEBA – PCP

AMIDONE – methadone

AMP – amphetamine

AMPING – to have accelerated heartbeat

AMT – dimethyltryptamine

ANGEL – PCP

ANGEL DUST – PCP

Drug slang & street terms

ANGEL TEARS – liquid LSD
ANGELS IN THE SKY – LSD
ANGIE – cocaine
ANGOLA – marijuana
ANIMAL – LSD
ANTIFREEZE – heroin
AUNT HAZEL – heroin
AUNT MARY – marijuana
AUNT NORA – cocaine
AUNTIE – opium
AUNTIE EMMA – opium
AURORA BOREALIS – PCP
B-40 – a cigar laced with marijuana (a blunt) and dipped in malt liquor
BABY SLITS – MDMA
BABY T – crack
BABYSIT – to guide someone through their first drug experience
BACKBREAKERS – LSD cut with strychnine
BAD BUNDLE – inferior quality heroin
BAD TRIP – a bad acid trip
BAG – a container for drugs (especially marijuana)
BAG MAN – a person who transports drug money
BAKED – to be under the influence of a drug (high, stoned)
BALE – marijuana
BALL – crack
BALLOON – a heroin supplier
BALLOT – heroin
BAM – a depressant; an amphetamine
BANG – to inject a drug

BARB - a depressant; a barbiturate

BARBIES - depressants

BARRELS - LSD

BART SIMPSONS - a dose of LSD on blotter paper bearing an image of the cartoon character Bart Simpson

BASE - cocaine; crack; a freebase

BASEBALL - crack

BATTERY ACID - LSD

BAZOOKA - cocaine; crack

BEAM ME UP SCOTTIE - crack dipped in PCP

BEAMER - a crack user

BEANS - amphetamines; depressants

BEAST - LSD

BEIGING - to chemically alter the color of cocaine to make it appear of a higher purity than it is

BELT - the effects of a drug

BELUSHI - cocaine and heroin

BENDER - a long period of heavy substance use, usually after a long period of abstinence

BENNIE - an amphetamine

BENZ - an amphetamine

BERNIE - cocaine

BIG BAG - heroin

BIG BLOKE - cocaine

BIG C - cocaine

BIG D - LSD

BIG FLAKE - cocaine

BIG H - heroin

BIG HARRY - heroin

Drug slang & street terms

BIG O – opium

BING – a portion of a drug that is enough for one injection

BINGO – to inject a drug

BINGS – crack

BIZ – a bag, or portion, of drugs

BLACK – opium; marijuana

BLACK ACID – LSD; LSD and PCP

BLACK AND WHITE – an amphetamine

BLACK BART – marijuana

BLACK BEAUTIES – depressants; amphetamines

BLACK BIRDS – an amphetamine

BLACK BOMBERS – an amphetamine

BLACK BUTTON – a dried button of peyote

BLACK GANGA – marijuana resin

BLACK GOLD – high-potency marijuana

BLACK HASH – opium and hashish

BLACK MOLLIES – an amphetamine

BLACK MOTE – marijuana mixed with honey

BLACK PEARL – heroin

BLACK POWDER – black hashish ground into a powder

BLACK ROCK – crack

BLACK RUSSIAN – hashish laced with opium

BLACK STAR – LSD

BLACK STUFF – heroin

BLACK SUNSHINE – LSD

BLACK TABS – LSD

BLACK TAR – heroin

BLACKBIRD – a type of LSD

BLACKS – amphetamines

BLAST – to smoke marijuana; to smoke crack

BLAST A JOINT – to smoke marijuana

BLAST A ROACH – to smoke marijuana (especially a "roach", or butt of a marijuana cigarette)

BLAST A STICK – to smoke marijuana (especially a marijuana cigarette)

BLASTED – to be under the influence of a drug

BLAZE – to smoke marijuana

BLIND SQUID – ketamine; LSD

BLITZED – to be under the influence of a drug

BLOCKBUSTERS – depressants

BLONDE – marijuana

BLOTTER – a piece of blotter paper soaked in LSD; a dose of LSD

BLOTTER ACID – LSD distributed on blotter paper

BLOW – cocaine; to snort cocaine; to smoke marijuana

BLOW A FIX – when an injection misses the vein and is wasted in the skin

BLOW A SHOT – when an injection misses the vein and is wasted in the skin

BLOW A STICK – to smoke marijuana (especially a marijuana cigarette)

BLOW BLUE – to snort cocaine

BLOW COKE – to snort cocaine

BLOW SMOKE – to snort cocaine

BLOW THE VEIN – when an injection misses the vein and is wasted in the skin

BLOWCAINE – crack diluted with cocaine

BLOWING SMOKE – marijuana

BLOWN – to be high on marijuana

BLUE ACID – LSD

Drug slang & street terms

BLUE ANGELS – a depressant
BLUE BARRELS – LSD
BLUE BIRDS – a depressant
BLUE BOY – an amphetamine
BLUE BULLETS – a depressant
BLUE CAPS – mescaline
BLUE CHAIRS – LSD
BLUE CHEERS – LSD
BLUE HEAVEN – LSD
BLUE HEAVENS – a depressant
BLUE HERO – heroin
BLUE MICRODOT – LSD
BLUE MIST – LSD
BLUE MOONS – LSD
BLUE SAGE – marijuana
BLUE SKY BLOND – a high potency marijuana from Colombia
BLUE STAR – LSD; PCP
BLUE TIPS – a depressant
BLUE VIALS – LSD
BLUNT – a cigar laced with marijuana
BOAT – marijuana laced with PCP
BOMB – crack; heroin; high potency heroin; a large marijuana cigarette
BOMBER – a marijuana cigarette
BONES – crack
BONG – a water pipe used to smoke marijuana
BOOST AND SHOOT – to steal in order to support a drug habit
BOOSTER – to snort cocaine
BOOT – to inject a drug

A PARENT'S GUIDE TO STREET DRUGS

BOOT THE GONG – to smoke marijuana

BOOTED – to be under the influence of a drug

BOOTY JUICE – MDMA dissolved in a liquid

BOTRAY – crack

BOTTLES – crack vials; amphetamines

BOULDER – crack; a twenty-dollar portion of crack

BOULYA – crack

BOUNCING POWDER – cocaine

BOWL – 1/32 or 1/16 ounce of marijuana; a small pipe used to smoke marijuana

BOY – heroin

BRAIN TICKLERS – amphetamines

BUTT NAKED – PCP

BUTTER – marijuana; crack

BUTTER FLOWER – marijuana

BUTTONS – (peyote) mescaline

BUY SOME CHEESE – to buy hashish

BUZZ – to be under the influence of a drug

BUZZED – to be high on drugs

C – cocaine

C&M – cocaine and morphine

C.W. – "completely wrecked", to be very high on a drug

CACTUS – (peyote) mescaline

CACTUS BUTTONS – (peyote) mescaline

CACTUS HEAD – (peyote) mescaline

CADILLAC – PCP

CAINE – cocaine; crack

CAKES – round discs of crack

CALIFORNIA SUNSHINE – LSD

Drug slang & street terms

CAM TRIP – a high potency marijuana

CAMBODIAN RED/CAM RED – marijuana from Cambodia

CAME – cocaine

CAN – marijuana; 1 ounce of a drug

CANADIAN BLACK – marijuana

CANDY C – cocaine

CANNON – a large marijuana cigarette

CANOE – a marijuana cigarette with a hole in its side (resembles a canoe)

CAP – crack; LSD; a portion of crystal methamphetamine

CAP UP – to transfer bulk form drugs to capsules

CAPITAL H – heroin

CAPS – crack; heroin

CARRIE NATION – cocaine

CATNIP – marijuana

CAVIAR – crack

CAVITIES – pin-prick marks left on the skin from repeated needle injections

C-DUST – cocaine

CECIL – cocaine

CEREAL – marijuana that is smoked in a pipe

C-GAME – cocaine

CHALK – methamphetamine; amphetamine

CHALKING – to chemically alter the color of cocaine so it looks white, and appears of a higher purity than it is

CHAMBER – a pipe used to smoke marijuana

CHANNEL – a vein into which a drug is injected

CHANNEL SWIMMER – an intravenous heroin user

CHARGE – marijuana

CHARGED UP – to be under the influence of a drug

CHARLEY – heroin

CHARLIE – cocaine

CHASE – to smoke cocaine; to smoke marijuana

CHASER – a compulsive crack user

CHASING THE DRAGON – crack and heroin

CHASING THE TIGER – to smoke heroin

CHAZE – to use a new pipe for the first time

CHEAP BASING – to use crack

CHECK – a personal supply of drugs (stash)

CHEMICAL – crack

CHEWED – to be very high on marijuana or hashish

CHICAGO BLACK – marijuana

CHICAGO GREEN – marijuana

CHICKEN POWDER – an amphetamine

CHICKEN SCRATCH – to search on ones hands and knees for crack

CHICKEN-HEAD – a cocaine addict

CHICLE – heroin

CHIEF – LSD; (peyote) mescaline

CHIEVA – heroin

CHINA CAT – high-potency heroin

CHINCHE – heroin

CHINESE DRAGONS – LSD

CHINESE MOLASSES – opium

CHINESE RED – heroin

CHINESE TOBACCO – opium

CHIP – heroin

CHIPPIE – marijuana

CHIPPING – the occasional use of drugs

•••••
Drug slang &
street terms

· · · ·
Drug slang & street terms

CHIPPY – cocaine

CHIRA – marijuana

CHOCOLATE – opium; an amphetamine

CHOCOLATE CHIPS – MDMA

CHOKER – a large or powerful dose (hit) of crack

CHOLLY – cocaine

CHORALS – a depressant

CHRISTINA – an amphetamine

CHRISTINE – crystal methamphetamine

CHRISTMAS ROLLS – a depressant

CHRISTMAS TREE – marijuana; a depressant; an amphetamine

CHRONIC – marijuana; marijuana laced with crack

CHUCKS – the hunger caused by heroin withdrawal

CHURCH – a dose of LSD on blotter paper bearing an image of a cross

CID – LSD

CIGARETTE PAPER – a packet of heroin

CJ – PCP

C-JOINT – a place where cocaine is sold

CLARITY – MDMA

CLEAR UP – to stop using drugs

CLICKER – crack and PCP

CLIFFHANGER – PCP

CLIMAX – crack; heroin

CLIMB – a marijuana cigarette

CLIPS – rows of drug vials that are heat-sealed together

CLOCKING PAPER – to make a profit from selling drugs

CLOUD – crack; a large dose (hit) of crack taken from a pipe

COASTING – to be under the influence of a drug

COASTS TO COASTS – amphetamines

COCA – cocaine

COCAINE BLUES – the depression that accompanies extended cocaine use

COCHORNIS – marijuana

COCKTAIL – a cigarette laced with cocaine or crack; a partially smoked marijuana cigarette inserted into a tobacco cigarette

COCO ROCKS – dark brown crack made by adding chocolate pudding during production

COCO SNOW – a kind of cut crack

COCO PUFF – to smoke cocaine and marijuana

COCONUT – cocaine

COFFEE – LSD

COFFEE CUPS – bags used to hold marijuana

COKE – cocaine; crack

COKE BAR – a bar where cocaine is openly used

COLA – cocaine

COLD TURKEY – to quit using drugs altogether

COLOMBIAN – marijuana

COLUMBO – PCP

COLUMBUS BLACK – marijuana

CONNECT – to purchase drugs

CONTACT LENS – LSD

COOK – to prepare a powdered drug for injection by mixing it with water and heating it, transforming it into a liquid

COOK DOWN – to liquify a powdered drug by mixing it with water and heating it

COOKIES – crack rocks

COOLER – a cigarette laced with a drug

COP – to acquire drugs (e.g., "I'll cop a gram")

• • • •
Drug slang & street terms

Drug slang & street terms

CO-PILOT – an amphetamine

CORRINNE – cocaine

COTTON BROTHERS – cocaine, heroin, morphine

COURAGE PILLS – heroin; a depressant

COZMO'S – PCP

CRACK – a potent, crystallized form of cocaine; a ready-to-smoke freebase, or boiled residue of cocaine powder cut with ammonia or baking soda

CRACK GALLERY – a place where crack is bought and sold

CRACKHEAD – a person who smokes crack

CRACK SPOT – a place crack is bought and sold

CRACKER JACKS – people who smoke crack

CRACKERS – LSD

CRANK – methamphetamines; amphetamines

CRANKING UP – to inject a drug

CRAZY COKE – PCP

CRAZY EDDIE – PCP

CRAZY WEED – marijuana

CREEPER BUD – marijuana that has intense delayed effects

CRINK – methamphetamines

CRIP – crystal methamphetamine

CRIPPLE – a marijuana cigarette

CRIPPY – strong marijuana; marijuana laced with crack

CRIS – methamphetamines

CRISCO – crystal methamphetamine

CRISSCROSS – amphetamines

CRISSY – crystal methamphetamine

CHRISTINA – methamphetamines

CHRISTY – smokable methamphetamines

CROAK - crack and a methamphetamine

CROSS TOPS - amphetamines

CROSSROADS - amphetamines

CROW - cocaine

CROWN CRAP - heroin

CRUMBS - tiny crystal rock pieces of crack

CRUMB SNATCHER - a junkie who steals tiny crystal rock pieces of crack

CRUNCH and MUNCH - crack

CRUSTY TREATS - cocaine

CRUZ - opium from Veracruz, Mexico

CRYING WEED - marijuana

CRYPTO - a methamphetamine

CRYSTAL - crystal methamphetamine; PCP; cocaine

CRYSTAL JOINT - PCP

CRYSTAL METH - a solid, smokable form of methamphetamine called crystal methamphetamine

CRYSTAL POP - cocaine and PCP

CRYSTAL T - PCP

CRYSTAL TEA - LSD

CUBE - 1 ounce of a drug; a dose of LSD in a sugar cube

CUPCAKES - LSD

CUSHION - a vein into which a drug is injected

CUT-DECK - heroin cut, or diluted, with powdered milk

CYCLINE - PCP

CYCLONES - PCP

D.L. SPOT - a "safe" place where drugs are sold, bought and used

DADDY - a marijuana cigarette

DANK - marijuana

Drug slang & street terms

DAWAMESK – marijuana

DEAD ON ARRIVAL (DOA) – PCP; crack; heroin

DEALER – a person who sells drugs

DECADENCE – MDMA

DECK – 1 to 15 grams of heroin, also known as a bag; a packet of drugs

DEEDA – LSD

DEMO – a small, sample-sized quantity of crack

DEMOLISH – crack

DENTAL FLOSS – LSD

DETROIT PINK – PCP

DEUCE – a two-dollar portion of a drug; heroin

DEVIL'S SMOKE – crack

DEVIL'S DANDRUFF – powdered cocaine

DEVIL'S DICK – a crack pipe

DEW – marijuana; the oily residue that remains in a pipe after it has been used for smoking base

DEWS – a ten-dollar portion of a drug

DEXIES – amphetamines

DIABLO – a dose of LSD on blotter paper bearing an image of the devil

DIAMBISTA – marijuana

DIESEL – heroin

DIET PILLS – amphetamines

DIME – 1/16 ounces of marijuana

DIME – crack; a ten-dollar portion of crack

DIME BAG – a ten-dollar portion of a drug (especially marijuana)

DIME'S WORTH – a dose of heroin large enough to cause death

DING – marijuana

DIP – crack; a cigarette dipped in embalming fluid

DIPPER – PCP

DIPPING OUT – a person who delivers crack (crack runner) who takes some of the drug that is being delivered

DIRGE – PCP

DIRT – heroin

DIRT GRASS – inferior quality marijuana

DIRTY BASING – crack

DISCO BISCUITS – depressants

DISEASE – a person's preferred drug

DITCH – marijuana

DITCH WEED – inferior quality marijuana from Mexico

DIVIDER – to share a marijuana cigarette with another person

DO A BOWL – to smoke marijuana from a pipe

DO A LINE – to snort cocaine

DO IT JACK – PCP

DOA (DEAD ON ARRIVAL) – PCP; crack; heroin

DOCTOR – MDMA

DOG FOOD – heroin

DOGGIE – heroin

DOLLAR – a hundred-dollar portion of a drug

DOLLS – depressants

DOMESTIC – marijuana that is grown locally

DOMINOES – amphetamines

DONNA JUANITA – marijuana

DOPE – a generic term for any drug

DOPE FIEND – a drug addict

DOTS – LSD; (peyote) mescaline

DOUBLE BUBBLE – cocaine

DOUBLE CROSS – an amphetamine

DOUBLE TROUBLE – a depressant

• • • • •
Drug slang &
street terms

Drug slang & street terms

DOUBLE UPS – a twenty-dollar piece of crack that can be broken into two twenty-dollar pieces
DOUBLE YOKE – crack
DOVE – a thirty-five dollar piece of crack
DOWNER – a depressant
DOWNTOWN – heroin
DOWNTOWN BROWN – inferior quality marijuana
DRAW UP – to inject a drug
DREAM – cocaine
DREAM GUM – opium
DREAM STICK – opium
DREAMER – morphine
DREAMS – opium
DRECK – heroin
DRINK – PCP
DROWSY HIGH – a depressant
DRY HIGH – marijuana
DUB SACK – a twenty-dollar portion of a drug (especially marijuana)
DUCT – cocaine
DUMMY DUST – PCP
DUROS – marijuana
DUST – a powdered drug; heroin; cocaine; PCP; marijuana cut with a chemical
DUST JOINT – a marijuana cigarette laced with PCP
DUST OF ANGELS – PCP
DUSTED – to be under the influence of PCP (high)
DUSTED PARSLEY – marijuana laced with PCP
DUSTING – to lace marijuana with another drug (especially PCP, heroin, or cocaine)

DYNAMITE – heroin and cocaine
DYNO – heroin
DYNO-PURE – heroin
E (Ecstasy, XTC) – MDMA
EARTH – a marijuana cigarette
EASY SCORE – to easily obtain a drug
EAT – to ingest LSD
EATING – to ingest a drug
E-BALL – a type of ecstasy with an eight ball on it
ECSTASY – MDMA
EIGHT BALL – 1/8 ounces of a drug
EIGHTBALL – crack and heroin
EIGHTH – a portion of heroin or marijuana
EL CID – LSD
EL DIABLO – marijuana; cocaine and heroin
EL GATO DIABLO – crystal methamphetamine
ELAINE – MDMA
ELBOW – a pound of marijuana
ELECTRIC KOOL AID – LSD
ELLE MOMO – marijuana laced with PCP
ELLIS DAY – LSD
EMBALMING FLUID – PCP
ENDO – marijuana
ENERGIZER – PCP
ESRA – marijuana
ESSENCE – MDMA
EUPHORIA – MDMA; (peyote) mescaline; crystal methamphetamine
EXPLORERS CLUB – a group of LSD users
EYE OPENER – crack; an amphetamine

• • • • •
Drug slang &
street terms

Drug slang & street terms

FACTORY – a place where drugs are manufactured, cut, and/or diluted
FADED – to be under the influence of marijuana (high, stoned)
FAT BAGS – crack
FAT PAPPY – a large marijuana cigarette or blunt
FATTY – a marijuana cigarette
FEED BAG – a container for marijuana
FIFTY-ONE – crack
FIRE – to inject a drug; crack and methamphetamine
FIRE IT UP – to smoke marijuana
FIRST LINE – morphine
FISH SCALES – crack
FIVE CENT BAG – a five-dollar portion of a drug
FIVE DOLLAR BAG – a fifty-dollar portion of a drug
FIVE SACK – a five-dollar portion of marijuana
FIVES – amphetamines
FIX – to inject a drug; a dose of a drug
FIZZIES – methadone
FLAKE – cocaine
FLAKES – PCP
FLAME COOKING – to smoke a cocaine base (freebase) by placing the pipe over a gas stove flame
FLAMETHROWERS – a cigarette laced with cocaine and heroin
FLASH – LSD
FLASHERS – LSD that is very hallucinogenic
FLAT BLUES – LSD
FLEA POWDER – low-purity heroin
FLORIDA SNOW – cocaine
FLY MEXICAN AIRLINES – to smoke marijuana
FLYING – to be under the influence of a drug (high, stoned)

FLYING TRIANGLE – a type of LSD

FOILERS – to smoke cocaine on a piece of tin foil

FOLLOWING THAT CLOUD – to search for a drug

FOOLISH POWDER – heroin; cocaine

FOOTBALLS – amphetamines

FORWARDS – amphetamines

FREEBASE – a boiled residue of cocaine powder cut with ammonia or baking soda for smoking; to smoke a freebase

FREEZE – cocaine; to renege on a drug deal

FRENCH BLUE – an amphetamine

FRENCH FRIES – crack

FRESH – PCP

FRESH KILL – to steal another person's drugs

FRIES – crack

FRISCO SPECIAL – cocaine, heroin and LSD

FRISCO SPEEDBALL – cocaine, heroin and LSD

FRISKIE POWDER – cocaine

FRY – crack or marijuana laced with embalming fluid or acid

FRY DADDY – crack and marijuana; a cigarette laced with crack

FRYING – to be under the influence of LSD

FUEL – marijuana laced with an insecticide; PCP

FUTURE – crystal methamphetamine

G – 1 gram of a drug

GALLOPING HORSE – heroin

GANGSTER – marijuana

GARBAGE ROCK – crack

GEE – opium

GEEK – crack and marijuana

GEEKER – a crack user

Drug slang & street terms

Drug slang & street terms

GEEZE – to snort cocaine

GEEZER – to inject a drug

GEEZIN A BIT OF DEE GEE – to inject a drug

GEL CAPS – a form of LSD

GEL TABS – a form of LSD

GEORGE SMACK – heroin

GET A GAGE UP – to smoke marijuana

GET LIFTED – to be under the influence of drugs

GET NICE – to be under the influence of drugs; to "get high"

GET OFF – to inject a drug; to "get high"

GHB – gamma hydroxybutyrate

GHOST – LSD

GIGGLE SMOKE – marijuana

GIMMICK – the equipment used to inject a drug

GIMMIE – crack and marijuana

GIN – cocaine

GIVE WINGS – to inject a person with heroin; to teach a person how to inject a drug (especially heroin)

GLAD STUFF – cocaine

GLASS – hypodermic syringe; an amphetamine

GLASS GUN – a hypodermic syringe

GLASSES – a glass pipe

GO INTO A SEWER – to inject a drug

GO LOCO – to smoke marijuana

GO ON A SLEIGH RIDE – to snort cocaine

GOD'S DRUG – morphine

GOD'S MEDICINE – opium

GOING TO MEET SID (OR SIDNEY) – to purchase LSD

GOLD DUST – cocaine

GOLD STAR – marijuana

GOLDEN DRAGON – LSD

GOLDEN GIRL – heroin

GOLDEN LEAF – very high-quality marijuana

GOLF BALL – crack

GONDOLA – opium

GONG – marijuana; opium

GONG RINGER – a large marijuana cigarette

GOOD – PCP

GOOD AND PLENTY – heroin

GOOD BUTT – a marijuana cigarette

GOOD GIGGLES – marijuana

GOOD GO – to receive the proper amount of drugs for the price

GOOD H – heroin

GOOD LICK – a quality drug

GOOFBALL – cocaine and heroin; a depressant

GOOFERS – depressants

GOOFY'S – LSD

GOPHER – a person who delivers drugs

GORIC – opium

GORILLA BISCUITS – PCP

GORILLA PILLS – a depressant

GORILLA TAB – PCP

GRAPE PARFAIT – LSD

GRASS BROWNIES – marijuana or hashish baked into a batch of brownies

GRATA – marijuana

GRAVEL – crack

GRAVY – to inject a drug; heroin

Drug slang & street terms

Drug slang & street terms

GREAT TOBACCO – opium

GREEN BUTTON – a fresh dose (button) of peyote mescaline

GREEN DRAGONS – a depressant

GREEN FROG – a depressant

GREEN LEAVES – PCP

GREEN PAINT – marijuana

GREEN TEA – PCP

GREEN WEDGE – LSD

GREETER – marijuana

GRETA – marijuana

GRAY SHIELDS – LSD

GROCERIES – crack

G-ROCK – 1 gram of crack

GUM – opium

GUN – to inject a drug; a hypodermic syringe

GUTTER JUNKIE – a drug addict who relies on others to obtain drugs

H – heroin

H and C – heroin and cocaine

H CAPS – heroin

HACHE – heroin

HALF A FOOTBALL FIELD – 50 pieces of crack

HALF LOAD – 15 bags (decks) of heroin

HALF MOON – peyote mescaline

HALF PIECE – 1/2 ounce of heroin or cocaine

HALF TRACK – crack

HAMBURGER HELPER – crack

HAND-TO-HAND – the direct delivery and payment for a drug

HAND-TO-HAND MAN – a transient dealer who carries a small amount of crack for sale

HAPPY DUST – cocaine
HAPPY POWDER – cocaine
HAPPY TRAILS – cocaine
HARD CANDY – heroin
HARD LINE – crack
HARD ROCK – crack
HARD STUFF – opium; heroin
HARDCORE – a heavy drug user
HARM REDUCER – marijuana
HARRY – heroin
HASH – marijuana
HATS – LSD
HAVE A DUST – cocaine
HAVEN DUST – cocaine
HAWAIIAN SUNSHINE – LSD
HAWK – LSD
HAY BUTT – a marijuana cigarette
HAZE – LSD
HAZEL – heroin
HCP – PCP
HEAD DRUGS – amphetamines
HEADLIGHTS – LSD
HEARTS – an amphetamine
HEAVEN AND HELL – PCP
HEAVEN DUST – heroin; cocaine
HEAVENLY BLUE – LSD
HEAVY BITER – a person who has to take a large amount of a drug in order feel its effects ("get high")
HELEN – heroin

Drug slang & street terms

Drug slang & street terms

HELL DUST – heroin
HEN PICKING – to search on one's hands and knees for crack
HENRY – heroin
HENRY VIII – cocaine
HER – cocaine
HERB – marijuana
HERB AND AL – marijuana and alcohol
HERBS – marijuana
HIGH – the effect drug users feel when using drugs
HIGH OR LOW? – a phrased used to ask if a person wants to take a stimulant or a depressant
HIKORI – (peyote) mescaline
HIKULI – (peyote) mescaline
HIM – heroin
HINKLEY – PCP
HIROPON – a smokable methamphetamine; crystal methamphetamine
HIT – crack; a marijuana cigarette; to smoke marijuana
HIT THE HAY – to smoke marijuana
HIT THE MAIN LINE – to inject a drug
HIT THE NEEDLE – to inject a drug
HIT THE PIT – to inject a drug
HITCH UP THE REINDEER – to snort cocaine
HITS – LSD
HITTER – a small pipe that is designed to administer only one dose (hit) of a drug
HOCUS – opium; marijuana
HOG – PCP
HOLDING – to be in possession of a drug
HOMEGROWN – marijuana

HONEY BLUNTS – a cigar filled with marijuana (blunt) and sealed with honey

HONEY OIL – ketamine

HONEYMOON – the early stage of drug use before addiction develops

HOOK YOU UP – to give a person a drug

HOOKAH – a free-standing, large water-cooled pipe shaped like a vase

HOOKED – to be addicted to a drug

HOPPED UP – to be under the influence of a drug

HORN – to snort cocaine; a crack pipe

HORNING – heroin; to snort cocaine

HORSE – heroin

HORSE HEADS – amphetamines

HORSE TRACKS – PCP

HORSE TRANQUILIZER – PCP

HRN – heroin

HUNTER – cocaine

HUSTLE – an attempt to obtain drug customers

HYPE – a heroin addict; an addict

HYPE STICK – a hypodermic needle

ICE CREAM HABIT – the occasional use of a drug

IN – to be connected with a drug supplier

JAG – an extended period of drug-use (see also bender)

JOINT – a marijuana cigarette

JONESING – to crave a drug

JOY POPPING – the occasional use of a drug

JUICE – alcohol

JUNK – heroin

JUNKIE – an opiate addict

KEY – a kilogram

Drug slang & street terms

Drug slang & street terms

KICK – to stop using a drug (e.g., "kick the habit")

KILLER – a strong drug

KILLER WEED – strong marijuana; marijuana laced with PCP

KIT – the equipment used to inject drugs (especially heroin)

KICKBACK – a relapse into drug usage

LEAPERS – amphetamines

LID – 1 ounce of marijuana

LINE – a dose of cocaine arranged in a line on a smooth surface

LOAD – a large quantity of a drug

LOADED – to be under the influence of drugs or alcohol

MAINLINE – to inject a drug directly into a vein

MAINLINER – a person who injects a drug directly into the vein

MAN – police

MANICURE – to remove seeds from marijuana

MARY JANE – marijuana

MATCHBOX – a measurement for a small amount of marijuana

MERCHANDISE – drugs for sale

MESCALINE – peyote mescaline, a hallucinogen derived from the peyote cactus

MICRODOT – a tablet of LSD

MISS EMMA – morphine

MONKEY – a drug dependency; a kilogram of a drug

MULE – a person who delivers drug

MUNCHIES – the hunger that may follow marijuana use

NAILED – to be arrested

NARC – a narcotics agent

NICKEL BAG – a five-dollar portion of a drug (especially marijuana)

OD – a drug overdose

ON – to be under the influence of a drug

ON A TRIP – to be under the influence of a drug (especially a hallucinogen)

ON THE NOD – to be under the influence of a narcotic or a depressant

OUT OF IT – to be under the influence of drugs

PANAMA GOLD/RED – a potent marijuana grown in Panama

PAPER BOY – a person who sells heroin

PAPERS – cigarette rolling paper; small pieces of paper, used to make marijuana or tobacco cigarettes

PARSLEY – marijuana

PCP – Phencyclidine, a hallucinogenic drug

PEACE PILLS – PCP

PEANUTS – barbiturates

PEPSI HABIT – the occasional use of a drug

PEYOTE – peyote mescaline; a cactus from which the hallucinogen mescaline is derived

PICKUP – to purchase drugs

PIECE – 1 ounce of a drug

PINKS – barbiturates

PLANT – a hiding place for drugs

POKE – to inject a drug

POT – marijuana

POTHEAD – a marijuana user

RAINBOWS – barbiturates

RED DEVILS – barbiturates

REEFER – marijuana

RIDING THE WAVE – to be under the influence of a drug

RIG – the paraphernalia for injecting a drug

RIPPED OFF – to be robbed

ROACH – the butt of a marijuana cigarette

Drug slang & street terms

Drug slang & street terms

ROACH CLIP – any tweezers-like device used to hold a butt of a marijuana cigarette

RUSH – the immediate effect of a drug (e.g, "drug rush")

SAUCE – alcohol

SCAT – heroin

SCORE – to locate and purchase a drug

SCRIPT WRITER – a doctor who writes a prescription for a drug addict's faked symptoms

SET UP – to arrange to have a person arrested for drug possession, selling, et cetera

SHOOT UP – to inject a drug

SHOOTING GALLERY – a place where addicts inject drugs

SHOTGUN – to smoke marijuana by blowing smoke back through the joint into another person's mouth

SINSEMILLA OR SINS – a potent form of seedless marijuana that is grown in northern California

SKIN POPPING – to inject a drug under the skin

SMACK – heroin

SNORT – to inhale powdered cocaine through the nostrils

SNOW – cocaine

SNOW BIRD – a cocaine addict

SPACE CADET – a habitual user of marijuana

SPACED – to be unresponsive to one's surroundings because of the effect of a drug

SPACED OUT – to be under the influence of a drug

SPECIAL K – ketamine hydrochloride, once a general anesthetic for human and veterinary use, now a common street drug

SPEED – amphetamines

SPEED FREAK – an amphetamine addict

SPEEDBALL – cocaine and heroin

SPIKE – a hypodermic needle used to inject drugs

SPLIFF – a large marijuana cigarette

SPOONS – a kitchen spoon used to cook cocaine or heroin

STAR DUST – cocaine

STASH – a place where drugs are hidden; a personal supply of drugs

STEP ON – to dilute (cut) a drug

STICK – a marijuana cigarette

STIMULANTS – drugs that speed up the body's systems

STONED – to be under the influence of a drug (especially marijuana)

STRAIGHT – to not use drugs

STRUNG OUT – to be heavily addicted to drugs

STUFF – drugs

SUPERMAN – a dose of LSD on blotter paper bearing an image of the cartoon superhero, Superman

TASTE – a small sample of a drug

TOKE – to inhale marijuana or hashish smoke

TOOT – to snort cocaine

TOOTER – small, hollow straw-like tube used to snort cocaine

TRACKS – needle marks and bruises on the arms from repeated injections (track marks)

TRAP – a hiding place for drugs

TRIP – to be under the influence of a drug (especially a hallucinogen)

TURF – a location where drugs are sold

TURNED ON – to be introduced to a drug; to be under the influence of a drug (especially LSD)

TWEAKING – a severe state of crystal methamphetamine addiction characterized by twitches, paranoia, psychosis and violent behavior

UPPERS – stimulants

• • • • •
Drug slang & street terms

Drug slang & street terms

WACKY TOBACCY - marijuana

WASTED – to be under the influence of a drug

WEED – marijuana

WHITE – cocaine

WHITE LIGHTENING – LSD

WIRED – to be addicted to amphetamines or heroin

WORKS – the equipment used to inject a drug

YELLOW JACKETS – a barbiturate

YEN – a strong craving

ZIGZAG – a brand of cigarette rolling papers often used to make marijuana cigarettes

ZOMBIE – a heavy user of drugs

ZONKED – to be under the influence of a drug

NOTES

1. *http://www.usdoj.gov*

2. ibid

3. *http://www.nida.nih.gov/*

4. *http://www.medsch.ucla.edu/som/npi/DARC/*

BIBLIOGRAPHY

Addiction Medicine: Western Journal of Medicine, 152(5), May 1990.

Addictive Behaviors: Prevention and Early Intervention. Lisse, Netherlands: Swets & Zeitlinger, 1989.

Alcohol and Drug Abuse as Encountered in Office Practice. Boca Raton: CRC Press, 1991.

Alcohol Risk Assessment and Intervention: Resource Manual for Family Physicians. Toronto: College of Family Physicians of Canada,1994.

The Alcoholic Patient: Emergency Medical Intervention. New York: Gardner Press, 1992.

Allen, John P. and Maisto, Stephen A. and Connors, Gerard J. "Self-report Screening Tests for Alcohol Problems in Primary Care". *Archives of Internal Medicine,* 155(16):1726-30,1995.

AUDIT: The Alcohol Use Disorders Identification Test: Guidelines for Use in Primary Health Care. Geneva: World Health Organization Program on Substance Abuse, 1992.

Beauvais, Fred and LaBoueff, S. "Drug and Alcohol Abuse Intervention in American Indian Communities". *International Journal of the Addictions,* 20(1):139-171, 1985.

Blaine, Jack D., et al, ed. *Diagnosis and Severity of Drug Abuse and Drug Dependence.* Rockville, MD: NIDA, 1995.

Blondell, Richard D., ed. "Substance Abuse". *Primary Care: Clinics in Office Practice.,* 20(1), March 1993.

Bien, Thomas H. and Miller, William R. and Tonigan, Scott J. "Brief Interventions or Alcohol Problems: A Review". *Addiction,* 88(3):315-335, 1993.

Bois, Christine and Graham, Kathryn. "Assessment". *Case Management and Treatment Planning* . Toronto: Addiction Research Foundation, 1993.

Cannon, Timothy B. and Cannon, Dale S, eds. *Assessment and Treatment of Addictive Disorders*. New York: Praeger,1988.

Chemically Dependent: Phases of Treatment and Recovery. New York: Brunner/Mazel, 1992.

Clinical Work with Substance-Abusing Clients. New York: Guilford Press, 1993.

Cohen, Saul. *Treating Alcohol Problems: The Family Physician's Guide*. Regina: Saskatchewan Alcohol and Drug Abuse Commission,1989.

Conigrave, Katherine M. and Saunders, John B. and Whitfield, John B. "Diagnostic Tests for Alcohol Consumption". *Alcohol & Alcoholism*, 30(1):13-26, 1995.

Crosby, Linda R, and Bissell, LeClair and Reilly, Cyril A. *To Care Enough: Intervention With Chemically Dependent Colleagues: A Guide for Healthcare and Other Professionals*. Minneapolis: Johnson Institute Books, 1989.

Dennison, Sylvia J. *Diagnosing Chemical Dependency: A Practical Guide for the Health Care Professional*. Springfield, IL: Charles C. Thomas, 1993.

Devenyi, Paul. "Prescription Drug Abuse". *Canadian Medical Association Journal*, 132 (Feb. 1):242-243, 1985.

Drug Abuse Prevention Intervention Research: Methodological Issues. Rockville, MD: NIDA,1991.

"Drug Abuse Related to Prescribing Practices". *JAMA*, 247(6):864-866, 1982.

Estes, Nada J. and Heinemann, Edith, M. *Issues in Identification of*

Alcoholism in *Alcoholism Development, Consequences, and Interventions,* pp. 317-333. St Louis: Mosby, 1986.

Friedman, Alfred S. *Assessing Drug Abuse Among Adolescents and Adults: Standardized Instruments.* Rockville, MD: NIDA,1994.

Goldman, Brian. "Confronting the Prescription Drug Addict: Doctors Must Learn to Say No". *Canadian Medical Association Journal,* 136 (April 15):871-895, 1987.

Handbook for Assessing and Treating Addictive Disorders. New York: Greenwood Press,1992.

How to Use Intervention in Your Professional Practice: A Guide for Helping Professionals Who Work with Chemical Dependents and Their Families. Minneapolis: Johnson Institute,1987.

Innovative Approaches in the Treatment of Drug Abuse: Program Models and Strategies. Westport, CT: Greenwood Press, 1993.

Jarvis, Tracey J, and Tebbutt, Jenny and Mattick, Richard P. *Treatment Approaches for Alcohol and Drug Dependence: An Introductory Guide..* Chichester, UK: John Wiley & Sons,1995.

Kappas-Larson, Pat and Lathrop, Laura. "Early Detection and Intervention for Hazardous Ethanol Use". *Nurse Practitioner,* 18(7):50-55, 1993.

Mendelson, Jack H. and Mello, Nancy K. *Medical Diagnosis and Treatment of Alcoholism..* New York: McGraw-Hill,1992.

Miller, Norman S. *Addictive Psychiatry: Current Diagnosis and Treatment.* New York: Wiley-Lis, 1995.

Miller, William R. and Heather, Nick, eds. *Treating Addictive Behaviors: Processes of Change.* New York: Plenum Press,1986.

Nathan, Peter. "Alcohol Dependency Prevention and Early Intervention". *Public Health Reports,* 103(6):683-689, 1988.

Nuckols, Cardwell C. and Greeson, Janet. "Cocaine Addiction: Assessment and Intervention". *Nursing Clinics of North America*, 24(1):33-43, 1989.

O'Neill, John and O'Neill, Pat. *Concerned Intervention: When Your Loved One Won't Quit Alcohol or Drugs*. Oakland: New Harbinger Publications,Inc., 1992.

Saunders, John B. and Foulds, Kim. "Brief and Early Intervention: Experience from Studies of Harmful Drinking. *Australian & New Zealand Journal of Medicine,* 22(2):224-230, 1992.

Schuckit, Marc A. *Drug and Alcohol Abuse: A Clinical Guide to Diagnosis and Treatment*. New York: Plenum Medical Book Co., 1995.

Skinner, Harvey A. "Early Identification of Addictive Behaviors Using a Computerized Life-style Assessment". *Addictive Behaviors Across the Lifespan: Prevention, Treatment, and Policy Issues,* Baer, J.S. and Marlatt, G.A. and McMahon, R.J., eds, 88-110. Newbury Park, CA: Sage Publications, 1993.

Skinner, Harvey A. "Early Identification of Alcohol Problems". *Medicine: North America,* (Jan. 1991):1878-1881, 1991.

Skinner, Harvey A. "Spectrum of Drinkers and Intervention Opportunities". *Canadian Medical Association Journal,* 143(10):1054-1059, 1990.

Skinner, Harvey A. and Holt, Stephen. *The Alcohol Clinical Index: Strategies for Identifying Patients with Alcohol Problems*. Toronto: Addiction Research Foundation,1987.

Sobell, Linda C. and Toneatto, Tony and Sobell, Mark B., et al. "Alcohol Problems: Diagnostic Interviewing". *Diagnostic Interviewing*. M. Hersen and S. Turner, 155-188. New York: Plenum Press,1994.

Storti, Ed and Keller, Janet. *Crisis Intervention: Acting Against Addiction*. New York: Crown, 1988.

Walters, Glenn D. *Substance Abuse and the New Road to Recovery: A Practitioner's Guide.* Washington, DC: Taylor & Francis,1996.

Watson, Donnie W. "Prevention, Intervention, and Treatment of Chemical Dependency in the Black Community". *Health Issues in the Black Community,* Braithwaite, R.L. and Taylor, S.E., eds., pp 64-78. San Francisco: Jossey-Bass, 1992.

Werner, Mark J. "Principles of Brief Intervention for Adolescent Alcohol, Tobacco, and Other Drug Use. *Pediatric Clinics of North America,* 42(2):335-349, 1995.

Werner, Mark J. and Adger, Hoover. "Early Identification, Screening, and Brief Intervention for Adolescent Alcohol Use". *Arch Pediatr Adolesc Med,* 149:1241-1248, 1995.

Wilkinson, D. Adrian and Martin, Garth W. "Intervention Methods for Youth with Problems of Substance Abuse" *Drug Use by Adolescents: Identification, Assessment and Intervention.* Annis, Helen M. and Davis, Christine S., pp 5-22. Toronto: Addiction Research Foundation, 1990.

Williams, Etta. "Strategies for Intervention". *Nursing Clinics of North America,* 24(1):95-107, 1989.

INTERNET REFERENCES AND HELPLINES

While these links are good resources, I suggest you also go to the search engine of your choice and do your own Web search for groups and services active in your area. Please note that some of the following phone numbers do not work when calling from outside of the U.S. Check the Web site or in the Yellow Pages for a local phone number.

Alcohol and Drug Helplines (800) 821-4357
www.behavioralhealthonline.com

Boys Town National Hotline (800) 448-3000
www.boystown.org

National Drug Abuse Referral Info. (800) 262-2463
www.drughelp.org

Partnership for a Drug-Free America
www.ndpl.org

Mothers Against Drunk Driving (MADD) (818) 325-0235
www.madd.org

Ness Center, Council Domestic Violence Counseling (310) 360-8512
www.thenesscenter.com

Families Anonymous (800) 736-9805
www.familiesanonymous.org

Families In Action (770) 934-6364
www.nationalfamilies.org

Hazelden Foundation (800) 328-9000
www.hazelden.org

National Clearinghouse for Alcohol and Drug Information (800) 729-6686
www.health.org

References

National Crime Prevention Council (202) 466-NCPC
www.ncpc.org

Cocaine Helpline/Referral 1 (800) Cocaine
www.drughelp.org

Alcohol Helpline/Referral
1 (800)-ALCOHOL

People in Progress (213) 384-6689
peopleinprogress@usa.net

Community Anti-Drug Coalitions of America (800) 542-2322
www.cadca.org

National Council on Alcoholism and Drug Dependency (313) 861-0666
www.ncadd-detroit.org

National Stop Drugs Campaign
www.stopdrugs.org/identification.html